MMC

THE MUU-ANTIQUES

A NOVEL

SHOME DASGUPTA

The Muu-Antiques is a work of fiction etc.

ISBN: 979-8-9874654-3-1

Published July 2023 by Malarkey Books

Cover art by Mathew Yates

Interior design by Alan Good

malarkeybooks.com

For Mike B.

1

IN A WORLD FULL OF SMALLER WORLDS consisting of different sizes and shapes such as squares, triangles, circles, parallelograms, and oblongs, Percy found himself in the smallest world in his apartment above Macy Thorpewaite's garage. His place had nothing but a TV and a bed. That was all Percy needed. That was all Percy knew. It wasn't until Percy met Macy Thorpewaite, that he found another world full of muumuus and antiques and iced tea.

Macy raked the front yard—her back hunched over, sweat dripping from her forehead down to her rainbow-colored muumuu, and her untied black tennis shoes caused her to stumble from time to time. Percy sat in front of the garden full of blues, greens, oranges, and reds, pulling out the weeds. He wasn't a gardener. He didn't know anything about flowers and soils, and he had never used a lawn mower before he met Macy.

The Atlanta humidity stuck to their skin, and the pollen count was at its peak, leaving yellow dust on every car parked in their neighborhood. Percy sneezed and coughed and rubbed his eyes, hoping that Macy would give him a break and let him get some lemonade and pizza from the Bee And Bumble down the street. He rubbed his lower back, sore from bending over for long periods of time.

"Wipe your nose," Macy said. "It's dirty. What am I going to do with you, Penelope?"

She called him Penelope. From the first day they had met, she called him Penelope. He kept telling her that his name was Percy, but after a few weeks, he gave up on it, and it had been Penelope ever since. He became accustomed to it, and eventually liked it as it was the first time he ever had a nickname. Percy wiped his nose using the sleeve of his shirt.

"Tissue, Penelope," Macy said. "You are not four anymore, Penelope, you're twenty-four. An adult. Adults use tissues. I'm eighty-three. I'm the one who should be acting like a four-year-old."

"Can I get some lemonade?" Percy asked.

"If you must. But don't take too long—we have plenty to do today, Penelope."

She lit a cigarette and spat and looked at the front of her house. It was a bright white house with a blue door. The edges of the door were lined with dark red, and there was a window on each side of the house. The window on the left looked into the kitchen. The window on the right looked into the living room. Macy looked through the kitchen window and saw the sink was piled up with plates and cups and pans. She wiped her forehead and went inside.

When Percy returned from The Bee And Bumble, with a big smile and an even bigger cup of lemonade—it was the Super XXL size—Macy was sitting on the front porch, reading the newspaper. He sat down in a rocking chair across from her. The ceiling fan buzzed.

"Would you like some lemonade?" Percy asked.

"I don't think so, Penelope," she said.

"Back to the garden!"

"I don't think so, Penelope."

"How come?"

"I have a meeting to go to," Macy said.

"I can do it on my own."

"If I leave it with you, it'll look like some kind of archaeological dig site."

"Too true," Percy said.

2

M.M.C.

Terms Of Agreement

As a member of the M.M.C., I agree to:

1. Keep this organization a secret, and by breaking this accord, I understand that repercussions will ensue.

2. Pay for all items I've purchased, and by breaking this accord, I understand that repercussions will ensue.

3. Attend at least one event every month, unless an agreement has been made with the President at least a week prior to the event.

4. Wear a muumuu.

5. Muumuu.

6. Provide information about obtaining antiques.

7. Provide snacks and drinks if asked.

8. Use the underground paths provided by the M.M.C.

9. Pay in cash.

10. Have fun.

By signing this agreement, I will uphold all the rules stated above and any additional addendums from here on out. I understand what can happen if I do not abide by these rules.

Signature: Date:

_______________________   _______________________

3

Macy's husband, Zephyr, had died five years ago from respiratory problems. They didn't have any children. Percy felt bad for her, especially because she was old and alone. She rarely left the house or had any people over except for him. He believed that he was a younger male version of her, so they could relate to each other despite the difference in their ages. Percy, himself, was not a lonely person but lived a solitary life for the most part. Macy was his first friend since college, and he didn't spend time with anyone else. He loved the simple life, and waffles.

Percy walked through the fenced gate of Macy's house—the garden directly in front of the porch was full of tomato and squash plants. Every time he saw them, he wanted to grow some himself and live solely on the food he had produced from the garden. He tried to do it once, but he loved pizza too much, especially from The Bee And Bumble.

Zephyr, who had been an accountant, had saved enough money for Macy to live on her own after his death—between her husband's money and social security, Macy didn't have to worry about financial stability. Percy was in the process of getting his own financial stability started. He was able to get a job as a helper for the art professors at the University of Atlanta. He saw a posting for the part-time job the other day while walking by an art gallery and sent a résumé to the art department, and Allen, the director of the program, gave Percy a call a couple of days later. He hadn't started working yet, but Allen told him that he had gotten the job. Prior to getting this position, Percy's jobs included working at a funeral home, a hardware store, and a kebab hut. None of them really paid well, so he usually had to work more than one job to pay bills and eat. With this new job, he would only have to work at one place and he'd have holidays off.

He knocked on the door a couple of times before Macy came to open it.

"I need help with a light bulb in the kitchen," she said.

"The tulips look beautiful when they're blooming," Percy said.

"Come help me with the light bulb, Penelope."

"The pollen is thick today," he said.

They walked into the kitchen—the musky scent from the antiques she kept filled the house. Her place was full of old things. She flicked the light switch and nothing happened.

"I would try it myself, but I'm afraid I will fall if I use the ladder. Thanks for helping me out."

Percy followed her to the garage to get the ladder and took it into the kitchen. He couldn't figure out how to take the fixture off to replace the light bulb. Macy stood in the kitchen and watched him as he jiggled the casing for about fifteen minutes. Sweat formed on his forehead, and he felt like he was in P.E class, trying to do a pull-up while the rest of the class watched. He started to breathe hard, and his lower back started to hurt again.

"Would you like some water?"

He accepted her offer and took a break from trying to remove the light casing and stepped down from the ladder to sit at the kitchen table with Macy. He wiped the sweat off his forehead in disgust with himself. He felt like he was trying to build a house with his bare hands. At least I didn't have to do any pull-ups, he thought. After resting, he climbed back up the ladder and jiggled the fixture for a few more minutes until it finally came off. Dust fell from the casing onto his face.

"Cover your eyes, Penelope," Macy said.

Percy coughed.

"Would you like some more water?" Macy asked.

Percy gave a slew of sneezes.

"Would you like some tissues?" Macy asked.

He put the light bulb in and put the casing back on before he stepped down.

"Sorry to cause such a bother," Macy said.

"It was no problem at all," Percy said. "And it was great exercise."

"Well get some rest," she replied.

"Do you have any other light bulbs that need to be replaced? I think I'm pretty good at it."

"Sure you are, Penelope," Macy said.

4

Percy's apartment above Macy's garage was a pleasant place in a pleasant area—the houses in the neighborhood were enveloped by oak trees. There was a pond in the center of the neighborhood where children would throw pennies, teenagers would throw beer cans, and adults would throw fishing lines. The houses were antebellum in style, two stories, with pillars in the front. However, Macy's house was different from the rest—it was a one-story house with no pillars, and it didn't match the tone of the rest of the neighborhood. This had caused problems when Zephyr and Macy built it, but the neighbors became accustomed to the style of their house as soon as they tasted Macy's home-cooked apple pie covered in peach syrup. The main population of the neighborhood consisted of elderly people. Percy rarely saw any people around his age walking around the neighborhood, unless it was the holidays and families were visiting or it was summer time, and students would come home from college.

Percy had a dinner meeting with Allen—he wasn't too good at doing one-on-one dinners, especially with people he barely knew. He would say things he normally wouldn't say, and he would laugh at things he would usually not laugh at and most probably shouldn't laugh at. He would enter a whole new world, and become a whole new person. If Percy was a superhero, his name would be Captain Nervous—a man who has the ability to be nervous in any situation involving interaction with others. He wouldn't be able to have a sidekick because it would make him anxious having to be around someone all the time. This would be their first face-to-face meeting.

He walked into The Sea—the room was dimly lit, and each table had a candle placed in the center. Percy pulled out his wallet to make sure he had enough cash. It was thin—appetizers for dinner, he thought. He told the host, a man dressed in a black suit, that the reservation was under Allen Pritchard, and Percy followed him to the table where the professor was sitting.

"I thought I was early," Percy said. "Hope you weren't waiting too long."

"Would you like a glass of wine?" Allen asked.

As soon as Percy sat down, the waiter came, and Allen ordered a glass of white wine. Percy ordered a Coke.

"Are you excited about Monday?" Allen asked.

"Monday?" Percy replied. "I start Monday?"

"Sure you do. The former helper left this weekend for Florida. She told us Friday that she was leaving this weekend."

"Wow. I'm not sure if I'm ready to start Monday. I haven't even looked over any material yet."

"You're an art major right? You should know enough to get by, and then later on when you get some time, you can refine your lessons."

Percy wasn't an art major. He finished in General Studies because he generally didn't know what he wanted to study. He took one art class in college and made a B. In his résumé he had claimed that he had extensive experience with the history of art.

"Yeah. I guess I should be okay."

Percy was trying to remember if he had any art books at his apartment. But he wasn't sure if he had thrown them away, sold them, or kept them in some boxes. Allen explained to him what the job consisted of, and how the art department had a good batch of students who were interested in their field. Percy looked at Allen's hands the whole time because the professor did a lot of gesturing.

When their food came, Percy had already lost his appetite as he had consumed too much Coke and had eaten too many bread rolls. Allen ate roast chicken with rosemary potatoes, and Percy had ordered a small bowl of tomato soup and a plate of salad.

"Thanks for dinner, Allen," Percy said.

"I'll see you Monday then," Allen said.

It was almost eight o'clock. Percy was happy that he still had time to do something, but then he remembered that he didn't have any friends. Maybe when I start working at the college I could meet someone, he thought. He went back to the apartment to see if he had any art books on his shelf.

There were two large hardback art books. One was about Pablo Picasso, and the other was an overview of art. The former was Percy's favorite artist, and the latter contained all the classics for the most part. He thought that this would be sufficient enough to look at for the time being. Allen had told him that the seniors and juniors already had some paintings completed, and Percy figured that he could compare or relate their paintings to at least a few of the artists in the book, and then as time passed, he would learn more about their worlds. He just hoped that the students would not ask him to paint or draw anything, as he had yet to get past drawing stick figures.

5

Macy called Percy and asked him to go over to her place—she was excited and out of breath.

"Get your ass over here, Penelope," she said.

"My ass is going," Percy replied.

When he got there, she grabbed his arm and led him to the living room, which was full of antiques.

"Follow me, Penelope," she said.

She owned several vintage record players. None of them worked, but Macy used them as decoration. In front of a flower-decorated sofa was a cardboard box. She took out something covered in a gray cloth and held the object with both hands, putting it up to the light. She pulled off the cloth with the other hand and unveiled a model ship. It was on a wooden base and covered in a glass dome.

"This belongs to Zephyr's line of family," Macy said.

Percy had never met him, having met Macy after Zephyr had passed away, but she always talked about him.

"I think it was Zephyr's grandfather or great-grandfather who made this," Macy said. "He did it all by hand. It has been passed down from generation to generation. Zephyr loved it so much; he didn't want anything to happen to it, so he kept it under this cloth and placed it in a box for safekeeping."

"He must have had very still hands to do this," Percy said.

"I had completely forgotten about it. It has been packed for such a long time. And when I was going through this box of old things, I immediately remembered the ship once I saw the gray cloth covering it."

She said that she was going to clean the casing and place it on her shelf in her bedroom. She went to the kitchen to get some glass cleaner.

"I start a new job tomorrow," Percy said.

He explained to her what it consisted of, and Macy was pleased about it. She told him how she used to study art, and that she could help him out if he needed it.

"And you know, Penelope, if you ever need money I can always help you out. Don't be afraid to search for the sunken treasure in my house."

He went back to his place with Macy's iron to get all the crinkles out of his shirt and pants. Macy also gave him some rubber gloves to protect Percy from possibly burning himself.

"Would you like some goggles, Penelope?"

"I have some at the apartment," Percy said.

"Use starch."

"Carbohydrates," Percy said.

6

He got up early—he was supposed to be at the university at 7:30 in the morning, and he was finished getting ready by 6:30. To use up some time, he went to the Coffee And Kebab Shop, or CAB, as the regulars called it.

Everyone was always in a rush in the morning. They walked through the door and hurried to the counter, constantly looking at their watches, and as soon as they got their drinks, they would make a dash for the door. Percy never understood why everyone was in a rush. They could get up a bit earlier to beat the crowd, or go a little later after the crowd had died down, he thought. Percy wasn't the type of person to be in a rush and divide his days into minutes, seconds, and milliseconds. But I also don't have a life, he thought.

"They take forever," said the customer in front of Percy.

He turned his head toward Percy and shook his head, grunting.

"I just want a cup of coffee," he said.

"I kind of like the wait," Percy said. "It gives me time to slow down and reflect."

"Who the hell are you," the customer said. "Buddha?"

He continued to shake his head.

"I'm Percy," he said. "How are you?"

He stuck out his hand, but the customer snorted and declined to shake his hand. It didn't bother Percy, who had begun daydreaming about taking a trip to the zoo one day.

"Otters," he said.

The customer in front of him turned around and looked at Percy.

"What," he asked.

"What," Percy asked.

"Did you say something," the customer said.

"What did I say," Percy said.

"Otters," he said. "I think."

"They're so cute," Percy said. "I love otters. Do you?"

The customer turned back around, shaking his head again, and ordered his drink, and a few minutes later, Percy ordered a cup of coffee and bought the *Atlanta Chronicle*.

Prominent Atlanta Family's House Burglarized

On Tuesday, May 15, Leo and Jennifer Wright's house was broken into just a day before the Wrights returned from their vacation in Puerto Rico. Leo Wright, the CEO of Invest-Mints Incorporated, and his wife, Jennifer, were born and raised in Atlanta. There were no signs of forced entry. All of Mrs. Wright's jewelry is still there. No cash was taken. The 40-inch flat screen TV is still mounted on the wall. The computer iss still in the office. What was taken? Good question, reader. A vase. When asked about the vase, Leo states that "the vase is our most valuable possession, not because of its price, but because of its history. I wish they would have taken everything else. Everything else, but the vase." The vase, which was on its way to becoming a family heirloom, was first brought to the United States by Leo's father, Ted Wright. During his WWII tour, he had received the vase as a gift from the Zajacs, a family living in Poland during the war.

The vase is gold and silver, covered in gemstones such as garnets, rubies, emeralds, and sapphires to name a few. The Zajacs had received the vase as a gift from a politician in Poland by the name of Balta Bernard, whose daughter was able to escape the German insurgence with the help of the Zajacs. The Zajacs, in turn, gave the gift to Ted for helping them escape the war-torn country. The vase dates back to pre-WWI.

When asked for any last thoughts, Leo said, "Please return the vase. I won't press any charges, and if anyone knows about the burglary, there is a reward for any information."

Though the Wrights are well known for being one of the wealthiest families in Atlanta, they are also active within the community through donations, charities, and fundraisers.

Once Percy saw the students walking on campus, he became nervous. He never liked the campus atmosphere—too many people for him. Too many looks and glares. He always hated being late for class when he was in school. The whole class would divert their attention from the teacher to him, and he was afraid that he was going to run into something, or trip and fall. And then the teacher would stare at him to let him know that tardiness was unacceptable. This time, Percy was ahead of schedule and he made sure not to walk near any trashcans. He walked to the art department's office, where Allen was standing, talking to the secretary behind a counter.

"I didn't have the time to get in touch with you, but I have some bad news," Allen said. "The adjunct who was planning on leaving, decided to stay. They offered her a raise, and she decided to stay."

Percy wasn't sure if he was mad or not.

"Art," he said.

"Sorry I couldn't tell you earlier," Allen said. "I checked, but we really don't have any other positions available. I hope this doesn't put you in a bind."

"I'm not sure," Percy said.

"But I still have your résumé on hand, so if anything comes up, I'll give you a call."

Percy looked out the window and saw a student dressed in baggy black jeans and a white shirt covered in blots of paint.

"Picasso," Percy said.

7

Macy was watering plants in the front yard. A cigarette hung loosely from her lips and her eyes were almost closed so as to not let the smoke bother them. She was barefoot. Percy had rarely seen her wear any shoes apart from some house slippers from time to time.

"You remember that new job I told you about? Well, I didn't get it."

"I have many things that can be worked on at my place, especially the front yard, the back yard, and the garage. You've been helping me all this time, but without pay. I'll pay you as good as any other job. Or at least, enough to help you live comfortably. And in the meantime, Penelope, you can look for a more stable job if you need it."

"When can I start?"

"How about six in the morning, starting tomorrow? If you can get an early start, you won't have to be in the heat too long."

"I was awake at six in the morning today and bought a newspaper."

"I'll train you and you will learn gradually. Eventually, you won't need my guidance at all."

Percy sneezed.

"Tissue, Penelope," Macy said.

8

His first task was to toil in the front yard—watering the garden and yard, pulling out weeds, and rotating certain plants so that each plant could get total exposure to the sun. His lower back started to hurt again, and allergies were at full force as he worked in the grass. He fought through it, though, and performed each task with diligence though it took longer that expected.

After a couple of hours, he took a break and read the newspaper while drinking an iced mocha. He read the follow-up on the Wrights and their stolen vase.

The Wrights' Vase: Still Stolen

The vase, which was recently stolen from the Wrights' house, is still missing. Leo and Jennifer plan to raise the reward to $10,000. Leo asserts that "the house feels empty without it. We can take everything out—the furniture, the TVS and stereos, everything, and the house would feel the same way as it does now. Please return it to its rightful owners."

In a recent statement made by Jasper Barbs, Chief of the Atlanta Police, there has not been any progress with finding information about the vase; however, the department is continuing to search for any leads with great effort.

The Wrights were recently seen at the local Bowl And Barbeque Charity Event.

Macy sat with Percy on the porch and sipped the iced tea she had made for herself.

"I'm not working you too hard am I?"

"It's better than no work at all."

"I have bad nerves right now," Macy said.

She pulled out a pack of cigarettes and a lighter from her purse and lit a cigarette. She tilted her head back and blew the smoke out from her mouth. Her motions, from her hand to the cigarette to her mouth, all seemed natural. She looked younger with a cigarette in her hand, as if she was in her early twenties.

"You don't mind if I smoke do you?" she asked.

"Doesn't your doctor get on you for smoking?"

"I'm too old now to worry about these things. I should have worried about it when I was younger, but now it is too late."

"Ashes are pretty."

Percy asked her for a cigarette and felt like a thirteen-year-old who was trying to light a cigarette for the first time. It had been a few years since he had smoked and he became dizzy and tired after a couple of puffs.

"Have you heard about the Wrights?" Macy asked.

She picked up the newspaper. Percy took a sip of the watered down ice-mocha and told her that he had read about it yesterday.

"My husband and I were close to the Wrights. Their parents were good friends of ours. We all grew up together but went our separate ways as things happen. They were wonderful people. Gentle people. But Zephyr and I never knew their children."

She flicked her cigarette into the garden.

"Ted and Janet, the parents, had passed away four or five years ago. I think Ted had passed away first, and then about half a year later, Janet died. Amazing, how close we all were, and how it all faded away."

"Vase," Percy said.

"How about taking the rest of the day off," Macy said. "Have dinner with me."

Percy was surprised to hear Macy's offer. He didn't think she liked him too much, in spite of all the time they spent together. He showered and joined Macy for dinner. He took a small bouquet of flowers and a dress tie over to her house. He took the tie because he wanted to wear one, but he didn't know how to put one on. The flowers were from her garden.

"You look dashing," Macy said.

She had finished fixing the tie around Percy's neck. It was red with thin black strips. Percy wore it with a crinkled blue button-up shirt and brown pants.

"I never learned how to tie one," Percy said. "To be honest, there was never really an occasion."

"I can't remember the last time I ate dinner with someone," she said.

They sat in the dining room—lit by a double-tiered sparkling chandelier. Percy looked at her dining room décor—she had placed the model-ship in a cabinet across from where he sat. It was in the middle of china plates, teacups, and shiny forks and knives. She had cleaned the casing, which made the ship look brighter than before.

Macy placed some rice on his plate, and then some beef stew on top. She had also made corn and mashed potatoes.

"Any young ladies in your life?" Macy asked. "How come I don't see you with any friends? I know you're a quiet young man, but every now and then you should bring people over and have some fun."

"You're my only friend," Percy said.

"That's not good, Penelope," Macy said.

"I like to keep to myself for the most part," Percy said. "Other than spending time with you, I don't do much. Having dinner with the professor who didn't hire me was the last time I hung out with someone other than you."

"What about college," Macy said. "You went to college, right?"

"I had a couple of great friends during college, but we all went our separate ways just like you and Ted and Janet."

"That," Macy said, "I can understand."

He had to restrain himself from rushing the food into his stomach—he wanted to show some manners for Macy. She had taken a smaller helping than his, and ate slowly like she was counting every chew she took before swallowing. Each motion was thought out, from moving the fork from the plate to her mouth and back to the plate again. Her back was straight against the support of the chair. One hand held a fork while the other was neatly placed on her lap. Percy made sure not to put either of his elbows on the table. He tried to emulate her, but the rice would fall off the fork.

Percy looked at her face as she chewed her food and realized that she must have been a gorgeous lady when she was younger. He thought about Barbara Walters and Martha Stewart. They were both pretty women and must have been just as attractive when they were younger. Percy thought of Macy in the same way.

"Quit looking at me, Penelope," Macy said. "If you look at someone, you should say something too. It's awkward otherwise."

"I like Oprah," Percy said.

"She's okay, I guess."

As he finished his second serving, Macy asked him if he wanted another helping. Though he could have had another plate—home-cooked meals were rare to him—he declined.

Macy made some more tea and they went to the porch, where she started talking about her past. She looked up at the ceiling fan. Percy was used to seeing her as a stern and outspoken woman, but on the porch that night, he saw a different Macy—one who was feeling vulnerable.

"Zephyr and I met in 1942. But our friendship was soon interrupted as he went off to the War for a couple of years."

She puffed on her cigarette and sipped her tea. Percy was waiting for his tea to cool down.

"We all lived in the same neighborhood."

She continued to look up at the ceiling fan, and he looked at her neck. Macy didn't have too many wrinkles. Her neck was smooth, as well as her arms and face.

"There was Zephyr, Ted, Janet, Walter, Karey, Barlow, and Carl," Macy said. "We all grew up in the same neighborhood at the same time. We practically did everything together. I remember playing hopscotch on the street, and our parents would scold Janet, Karey, and me for jumping up and down in our skirts. We all would get in a lot of trouble for the things we did. And now that I think of it, we were ahead of our times. I think if we were growing up now, our personalities would have matched the present culture."

Percy fell off his chair and spilled some of his tea. Without looking at him, Macy handed him a napkin from her pocket.

"We smoked, and drank, and explored our curiosities at a very young age."

"Is that where Zephyr comes in?"

"Zephyr and I had a very peculiar relationship. We were good friends, but our physical relationship came far later, after we knew each other inside and out. I'll put him aside for right now. We would all sneak out and find the night spots, and somehow find our way in there, and have a good time. Luckily, we all looked older than we actually were. We would dance and dance until the room spun around us when we stood still."

Percy asked her for a cigarette and continued to listen to her reminiscing. The way she spoke, with her hands, and facial expressions, how she held her cigarettes and looked into the ceiling fan—she knew how to keep his attention. Percy coughed and used his hands to wave the smoke away from his face.

"The country was still getting over the Depression, the echoes of a future war were sounding in Europe, but we were oblivious to it all. We formed our own small country in our neighborhood, and it was wonderful."

She took a long drag from her cigarette and sipped her cup of tea, gazing into the round coffee table. She moved the cup in a circular motion as if she was gently swirling the liquid.

"And then Zephyr and the others went to the War," Macy said. "We still hadn't told each other how we felt for one another, and before I knew it, he was overseas. Though I didn't show it, I took it very badly. We were all still in the early processes of becoming adults, at that age of seventeen and eighteen."

Percy was interested in what she had to say, but he needed to get some sleep before starting another early day of work. He yawned and looked at the front yard instead of at Macy.

"I'm boring you with stories of my youth."

"Scars," he said.

"I guess I'll go get some sleep now," Macy said. "I'll understand if you are late for work tomorrow. It's already past midnight. You did a good job today, Penelope."

He thanked her for the nice evening and went back to his apartment. Before going to bed, he looked out the window and saw that Macy was still sitting on the porch. He watched her sit there for quite some time as she rocked in her chair and chain-smoked. She rarely looked anywhere else other than the ceiling fan. Percy didn't want to go to bed until he saw Macy go inside, which wasn't until about another hour later. He tried to fall asleep on the wooden floor, hoping that it would ease the pain in his lower back.

9

M.M.C.

Terms Of Agreement

Addendum 1:

No member of the M.M.C. will be allowed to discuss any matters pertaining to antiques, auctions, or muumuus during any sort of social gathering.

10

He was an hour late for work. He got ready and hurried out the door, but as he walked out, he noticed that the red light on the answering machine was blinking. It was Allen—he had called the night before. He wanted to go out to dinner again.

Macy had taped a piece of paper to the door of her house, which contained a list of the tasks she wanted Percy to perform for the day. It was mainly garage work. Macy had written down a list of things that she wanted to be thrown away, and there was another list that stated certain items that needed to be cleaned. Her garage was a never-ending cave, consisting of years upon years of saving everything that had come across her path.

"Rat pack?" Percy asked himself. "No, pack rat."

He sneezed.

The first item on the list was a medium-sized wooden cabinet. He shifted it from side to side to feel the weight—it wasn't as heavy as it looked. The wood was in good condition, and the door was still on its hinges. He carried the cabinet from the garage to the driveway. Macy was standing outside waiting for him.

"Sorry for being so late," Percy said.

"I got a killer hangover," Macy said.

"From the tea?"

"I put a little kick in mine," she said.

She wore a blue muumuu, sandals with red straps, and black sunglasses. Her hair was still messy from sleeping. She held a coffee mug in one hand and a cigarette in the other.

"So you want to throw away this cabinet?" Percy asked.

"You can throw it away if you want to, but if you want any of these things, take them."

"I'll keep this. I could use a little more furniture in the apartment. I just have a bed."

"I'll be inside. Come in if you get thirsty, Penelope."

After six hours of work, around one o' clock, Percy took a break and went to the coffee shop. He sneezed the whole way there. He ordered his drink and bought a copy of the *Atlanta Chronicle*. Skimming through the paper, he saw another article on the stolen vase.

The Wrights' Vase Has Yet To Be Found

There has not been any progress in finding the Wrights' vase.

Leo's most recent statement: "I really don't know what to do. It's amazing that the only thing that was taken was the vase. It's like it was an inside job. But who would take it? The only people who know the ins and outs of this house are me, my wife, and our dog, Jenkins.”

Chief of Police, Jasper Barbs states, “Somewhere, somehow, the case will come to light. Someone is going to make a mistake, and we can only wait. We have all of the pawn shops on alert, as well as surrounding museums and art collectors. There would be no other purpose for stealing such an item other than to sell it.”

To recap, the Wrights’ house was burglarized while they were on vacation, and the vase was the only item stolen.

Here is what locals are saying about the incident:

“I would just get another vase and put some flowers in it.”

—Jamar

“A vase? I would have taken the flat screen TV. To see C. Jones face up close and personal would be awesome. Go Braves!”

—Liza

“How much was it worth? Wow. I’d get the SWAT team to figure all that out.”

—Brian

“Why stop at the vase? I would’ve taken everything including the bathtub. I bet they have nice a bathtub. One with jet streams and all.”

—Amitra

"I've met the Wrights at a local fundraising event here. They are nice people. Good people. I wish I could find it for them but who knows where it could be. It could be in Australia for all we know, being used as a paperweight."

—Larry

When he got back to Macy's garage, he noticed how much different it looked from when he first peered into the cave of antiques. Macy was in the garage, looking through some of the boxes.

"The garage already looks a hundred times better," she said. "But it still needs some work."

Percy looked at the things he was taking to the apartment: the cabinet, a record player, two glass ballerina figurines, a painting of a ballroom scene, and a bust of Plato. Next, Macy wanted him to organize the rest of the things in the garage and place them against the wall. The heavier things were to be placed on the bottom, and the lighter items on top.

"Would you like this afghan?" Macy asked.

He looked at the multi-colored afghan she held in her arms and accepted her offer. The rest of the garage work wasn't too difficult. He finished around six. He knocked on Macy's door to let her know that he was done. She opened the door, dressed in all black, holding a pitcher of iced tea in one hand and two glasses in the other. It was the first time Percy saw her wearing something other than a muumuu. They sat on the porch and lit cigarettes.

"There was another article on the Wrights," Percy said.

"When Zephyr, Ted, Walter, Carl, and Barlow all came back, they each had something valuable given to them while they were in service. I actually forget what Carl, Barlow, and Walter had brought back, but everyone remembers the vase. It was such a beautiful thing, with the sparkles and colors. I do hope the Wrights find it."

"Do you keep in touch with any of the others that you grew up with?"

She looked up to the ceiling fan and blew a puff of smoke.

"For the most part, we haven't kept in touch in years. Zephyr and I remained friends with Ted and Janet because they lived in Atlanta and only a few streets away. But after they passed away, I only have memories of those friends. I have no clue where Barlow, Karey, Walter, and Carl are now. If I remember correctly, I had heard that Karey and Barlow were to be married, years ago. After they came back from the War, everyone went their separate ways. Barlow and Karey went to Florida. Walter to Virginia. And Carl, I think, moved to South Carolina."

Percy poured some more iced tea into Macy's glass and he finished off the rest.

"I don't know much about your past, but I am curious about what you want to do in the future. You're a young man, with a whole future ahead of you. You can't just work in my front yard for the rest of your life, Penelope."

It took him a few seconds to answer Macy's question because he didn't know what exactly he wanted to do.

"The future is coming," he said. "I'm bad at thinking ahead, so I guess that's why I like listening to your past. I've gone from job to job, and so far, I like this one the most. It doesn't take much to please me. I can get by with the essentials and a few extras, but that's about it. I mean, I do have dreams of becoming a millionaire and retiring early, and just relaxing the rest of my life, but I know it's not realistic. I do have a few ideas, though."

"Well, you never know," Macy said. "Sometimes, some things will just pop up in front of you and you've made it. But sometimes, you have to search hard and nothing will ever come. You never know."

11

Allen called Percy and apologized again for what had happened on the first day at school. They decided to meet at a small Lebanese restaurant.

"Would you like me to pick you up?" Allen offered.

"I'll just meet you there."

When Percy walked into the restaurant, there was no one inside except for the employees. He walked across the room and sat at a corner table. Five minutes later, Allen showed up. The waiter, Joe, went to their table as soon as Allen sat down. The restaurant was dimly lit as most of the light came through the transparent shades covering the windows.

"Hello, Allen. What would you like to drink today?"

Allen was a regular at the restaurant.

"I'll take a glass of Merlot please," he said.

Allen didn't look at Joe at all—he stood there for a few seconds, looked at Allen while giving a loud sigh, and walked away without saying a word.

Allen was dressed up. He wore gray slacks with a matching blazer, a white button-up shirt, and a red tie. Percy wondered if he had dressed up solely for their meeting, or he was coming from some other place where there was something important happening. Percy wore jeans, and a blue t-shirt.

"You look nice today," Percy said.

Allen looked at him with glassy eyes. Percy noticed the bags under his eyes, the wrinkles on his neck, and the loose skin on his cheeks. Joe came back with Allen's wine.

"I'll have the gyros and a plate of grape leaves," Allen said.

He closed the menu and placed it on the table.

Joe finished writing down their orders and sighed again as he walked away.

"Must be having a bad day," Percy said.

"Who?"

"The waiter."

"I didn't notice anything."

"He's been sighing a lot," Percy said.

He took a sip of his wine and offered Percy a sip.

"I'm fine with what I have," Percy said.

"How come you're here having dinner with me rather than your girlfriend?" Allen asked.

He leaned in.

"I don't think I have one," Percy said. "I mean, I don't have one."

Allen whirled his glass of wine and held it near his nose.

Joe came back with their dinners. He placed the plates on the corner of the table.

"Anything else?" Joe asked.

Allen took his plate and put it in front of himself. Without waiting for a reply, Joe walked away. As Percy reached over to his own plate, Allen had already taken a few bites of his meal. He wasn't taking time between each bite—he was eating as if he was a part of a contest.

Percy wanted to leave. He sat there and watched Allen chew on his grape leaves and listened to his hard breathing. He looked at his own plate, and there was about three-fourths of the gyros left.

"I wasn't as hungry as I thought," he said.

"I can eat everything here in one sitting," Allen said.

Joe came back to the table. It was the first time they had seen him since he gave them their dinners. He picked up their plates and placed the bill on the table.

"Aren't you going to ask us if we would like dessert?" Allen asked.

"Do you want some dessert?"

It was more like a statement than a question.

"I'm fine," Allen said.

Joe walked away.

"Excuse me," Allen said. "I must use the restroom."

He stood up and walked to the back of the building. While he was in the restroom, Joe walked back and picked up the ticket.

"Thanks," Percy said. "I don't need any change."

"He's evil," Joe whispered.

Percy looked around the room.

"Who?"

"Be careful, he toys with your emotions, as he did with mine today. Tomorrow, he'll be eating with your brother."

"But I don't have a brother," Percy said. "Do I have a brother? What have you heard?"

Without saying anything else, Joe zoomed off into the kitchen. Allen came back from the restroom.

"Are we ready?" he asked.

They walked out the door.

"I'm not doing anything else tonight," Allen said. "I was probably going to rent a movie—would you like to come over maybe and watch? Or we could go to your place."

"I think I'm just going to go home and get some sleep. Maybe some other time, though."

Percy felt bad—Allen seemed to be a lonely guy. Percy had felt lonely at times and wanted someone to talk to, but he didn't want to do anything for the rest of the night, being tired from the day's work. He scratched the back of his head and looked down at the sidewalk.

"So where did you park?" Allen asked.

Percy pointed at the 1995 Corolla in front of them.

"How's it holding up?" Allen asked.

"It's doing okay. As long as I change the oil regularly, and maintain the servicing."

"I'm parked right there," Allen said.

He pointed at a black Mercedes parked a few cars ahead of Percy's. Allen had just given it a good wash. Percy walked toward his own car and Allen followed. Percy stuck out his arm to shake his hand. Allen took a step toward him and started to caress the hair on the back of Percy's head. He tilted his head toward Percy's and made a movement forward, kissing him on the lips.

"Allen."

"Yes, Percy."

"I think I'm a heterosexual."

"Are you sure?"

"I'm a huge fan of breasts."

"Cool."

"But thank you—that's really sweet of you."

Allen ran his feet against the ground, in circles, making swirls of dirt.

I can't remember the last time I've been kissed," Percy said. "Thanks."

Allen smiled and looked down. Percy hugged him and they parted ways—when Percy got back to the apartment, he saw that only Macy's porch light was on and the rest of the house was unlit. He wondered why Macy had gone to bed so early as she usually stayed up well into the night, whether it was sitting on the porch or spending time in the kitchen. Somewhat worried, he walked over and knocked on the door. After there was no answer, he walked over around the side and peered through the kitchen window and saw nothing but darkness. He tapped on the window.

"Macy," he whispered. "Are you there?"

He went back on the porch and knocked again and waited for a few minutes before sitting on the rocking chair. It was the first time Percy didn't know the location of Macy, and he wondered where she could be as she was usually at home at night as long as he could remember.

12

Percy Winks
Curriculum Vitae

Education:

Bachelor's Degree, General Studies, University of Georgia, 2007
2.64 GPA

Experience:

I have studied art throughout my enrollment at the University of Georgia, learning about the history of painting and sculpting. I have also taken craft classes, learning about the brushstroke, and I have also taken a ceramics class. Though my GPA is average, I received an A in all of my art classes.

Grants, Scholarships, Honors:

I did not receive any grants or honors, but I received the Scholarship For Shelter Home Students (SFSHS), which paid for all of my tuition. If given the chance, I will work hard enough to receive grants and honors.

Employment:

Assistant Undertaker, Primm's Funeral Home—
Duties include dressing the dead and applying cosmetics.

Stocker, Renny's Hardware And Share—
Duties include shelving items in the hardware store, small and large.

Cook, KeBobby's Shed—

Duties include cooking some of the best kebabs in town. Check out their lunch specials—
totally worth it.

Usher, The Oscar—
Duties include tearing tickets, cleaning theaters, and telling customers to keep quiet.

13

"Where were you yesterday?" Percy asked.

"Yesterday?" Macy replied.

"Yeah, I got home after dinner and saw that all of the lights were out in your house. You're usually up. I got worried and knocked on the door a couple of times."

"Don't worry about me, Penelope," she said. "But if you must know, I was at the community center."

"Bingo?"

"No way," she said. "I don't like that game. It's boring and does nothing for my soul."

"So how come you went?" Percy asked.

"Don't worry about that," she said. "But I have some good news for you."

Macy gave Percy a week's paid vacation. Percy didn't want it, but she insisted on giving him a break for working so hard.

He didn't know what to do with his time off. He tried to watch TV, but he was too restless to stay still for more than twenty minutes. He didn't leave town, but he thought about the time he took a road trip to New Orleans with Bill and Monica while they were in college. They were all students at the University of Georgia at Athens. After they graduated they all lost touch with each other, but Percy liked to think they had a great time together when they were in school.

Monica, Bill, and Percy had worked at a sixteen-screen movie theater called The Oscar. That was where they met. They were all hired around the same time during the summer after their freshmen year. Bill was a tall and skinny guy during his freshman year, but by the time he graduated, he had gained a lot of muscle. Monica had the body of a track runner. She was shorter than Bill, but her long, tightly packed calves gave her a tallish appearance. They would watch movies together, and because they worked at the theater, they could watch any movie for free during the weekdays, when it wasn't crowded. They would usually go on a Tuesday, their day off, and they would watch movie after movie.

Movies were what led them to New Orleans. They decided to drive down there for the New Orleans Film Festival. They also went to the New Orleans Zoo And Aquarium. Percy loved the otters. They seemed to be in a state of enlightenment as they swam on their backs. He pictured them wearing sunglasses and lounging around in the water with some kind of bright tropical drink—the ones that come with a tiny paper umbrella.

Monica was Percy's closest friend back then. He almost fell for her. The main connection was that they both loved to laugh. Even when there was no reason to laugh, they would do so, and everyone would stare at them. They didn't care though because they were in their own world. As much as they liked to laugh, they also had the usual discussions about life, the future, and the past. They had a good mixture of everything. Monica was always there whenever Percy needed to talk about his childhood. She and Bill were the only people who knew about his orphanage upbringing. He didn't know his parents. He had no memory of them—his first memory was when he was three years old, and his mentor was feeding him peas. His parents were his older peers or his mentors and guidance counselors. Monica and Percy had similar tastes in movies and music. They were both fans of jazz. When they were in New Orleans, the three of them went to a café where live jazz music was being played, and they stayed there for hours watching the notes travel from the musicians' instruments into their own ears.

As long as Percy knew her, Monica was never in a relationship with anyone, and Bill would always try to get them together. But they never did because they both knew how serious they would get in such a short period. They weren't ready for such a commitment. At least, Percy would like to think so.

The thunder outside took Percy out of his reverie. He looked out the window and saw a gray Camry parked in Macy's driveway. He hadn't seen a car parked there since he had been living in the garage apartment. Percy washed up and went over to Macy's house. After a couple of knocks, she opened the door. She wore a bright orange muumuu with a matching hat.

"I have a visitor here," she said. "You'll be surprised to see who it is."

"Oprah?"

He followed her into the living room and saw an older-looking man sitting on the sofa. He wore gray slacks and a white button-up shirt. The first thing Percy noticed about him was the sparkling gold watch on his wrist, and his gray, slicked-back hair. He had an unlit pipe in his mouth.

"Remember all those stories of the past I've been telling you about," Macy said. "Well, the past is here. This is Barlow."

"I've heard many stories of you," Percy said.

"And all of it is true," he said.

"I'll go make some more iced tea," Macy said.

She went into the kitchen, leaving Barlow and Percy alone in the living room. He sat on the sofa, and Percy sat in a cushioned chair across from him. The coffee table separated them.

"How long will you be staying in Atlanta?"

Barlow took the pipe out of his mouth. His eyes were narrow and piercing.

"I decided to drive out here from Florida to see if I could find any of these old friends of mine. So far, Macy is the first I found."

He stuck his pipe back into his mouth and looked around the living room.

"Macy has a beautiful place here," he said.

"The kitchen light works great," Percy said.

Macy came back with a tray holding a pitcher of iced tea and some glasses. One glass was smaller than the others, and it was filled with Bourbon. She handed the half-filled glass to Barlow. Macy poured a glass of iced tea for Percy and for herself. Barlow took small sips of his drink and sighed after each swallow. Percy gulped down the iced tea.

"I guess I'll go get some sleep now," Percy said.

"It was nice meeting you," Barlow said.

"Do you have a place to stay?"

"I found a hotel on my way here," Barlow said. "It's not too far off. I've already dropped off my bags and checked in."

"You know you always have a place to stay in my house," Macy said.

"I'm sure the hotel will be just fine," Percy said.

Barlow laughed. Macy followed Percy to the door—he said bye to her and walked back to the apartment, but he made sure to pass by the Camry on his way. In it were two suitcases and a few bags. He wondered why Barlow had said that he had already checked into a hotel and left his baggage there when he still had them in his car. Instead of going back to his apartment, Percy walked to the side of Macy's house and sat down under the open kitchen window. It was hard for him to hear what they were talking about as they spoke in low voices and the thunder continued to crackle, but he could make out spurts of words.

"If you give me a bit of time," Macy said. "I think I can help you."

"I'm just in dire need," Barlow said. "I'm getting tired of this, and I don't deserve it."

Deserve what, Percy thought. The thunder clashed again, startling him.

"Just be patient," Macy said. "I can't directly help you with what you're looking for, but I might be able to help you in another way—give me until the end of the month."

Percy crouched, and peered over the windowsill, seeing Barlow and Macy leave the kitchen. Curious and confused, he walked back to his apartment just as the rain started to come down. He watched the rain slam against the window as he sat on the floor with his back resting against the side of the bed. He looked around his room as if it was the first time he had ever seen his own place and saw a drawing hanging on the wall, a picture of a sun and three stick figures on a playground. When he was at the shelter, one of Percy's friends had drawn it and given it to him. They hadn't kept in touch since his friend was adopted, but Percy was fond of the drawing, as it was the first gift he had ever received from another child at the shelter. The thunder clashed again, and Percy started to do jumping jacks.

14

"How was the visit last night with your friend?" Percy asked.

Percy was in Macy's kitchen—it was the day after Barlow's visit.

"It took me a while to realize what exactly was going on. Nowhere in my mind would I imagine that Barlow would be knocking on my door."

"He didn't take his suitcases out of his car," Percy said.

"He has changed quite a bit, but I guess after all these years, we all have changed. Bitter, but I don't know why. We're going out for dinner tonight."

"Have fun."

He asked Macy if he could start work again because he didn't have anything else to do. She insisted that he should still take the rest of the week off.

Percy looked at the three shiny purple-colored tin cups that Macy kept on the windowsill behind the kitchen sink. For as long as he had visited Macy, he had never seen those cups move or be used. He pointed at them and sneezed.

"Shut up," Macy said. "Bless you."

"How come?"

"How come, what?"

"The tin cups—how come? Percy asked. "Why don't you use them? They're pretty."

"Oh Penelope, where do I begin," Macy said.

She looked at her watch and pulled out a cigarette. It was the first time Percy saw Macy smoke inside of the house. The puffs of smoke gravitated toward the sink as she blew upwards. She sat down at the island, head leaning over the counter. Her other hand rubbed the temple of her forehead as she closed her eyes. Percy could tell that she was tired. He wanted to let her go and rest before dinner that night, but his curiosity for the tin cups prevailed.

"Where do you begin?" Percy asked.

"Before you existed," Macy said. "You wouldn't think it, but I had quite an eventful life. I can't remember if I told you, but I was a nurse's assistant stationed in France during WWII."

She went on to explain that after Zephyr and the gang left for the war, that she felt like she had a calling to go to the war as well.

"I volunteered," she said. "And I was sent to France, just east of Paris where Barlow, Walter, Carl, and Zephyr were stationed."

She took a deep drag and puffed as she continued to rub her forehead.

"Zephyr and I would exchange letters quite regularly," Macy said.

"A, B, F, H, R," Percy said.

"And that was how we became really close for we only went out on that one date before he left for the war."

Percy continued to look at the tin cups as Macy continued to blow the cigarette smoke up toward the ceiling. Various letters of the alphabet went through Percy's head.

"Purple," Percy said.

Macy put out her cigarette in her cup of tea and got up to spit into the sink. She picked up the three cups—the first time Percy saw them being moved. She went back to the island and placed them in front of her before taking one of the cups and running her fingertips around its rim. Percy looked at the ceiling lights and smiled, remembering the tough job of replacing the bulbs and his feeling of accomplishment after completing the task.

"I saw a lot while I was out there, Penelope. I used to be young and kind once, but the war changed me a good bit. I'm now old and bitter."

"You're great," Percy said.

"Quit it, Penelope."

Percy pictured her as a nurse and wondered if there were any photos of her from when she was young. Macy continued her story, recounting several of the injured soldiers she had to help.

"There was screaming," Macy said. "Lots of it. And amputations and looks of such despair that could never be forgotten. But at the same time, there were looks of relief and hope as some of the soldiers knew that they were going to be done with the war, regardless of lost limbs or permanent injuries."

Macy's voice became lower and lower as she talked. Percy felt like she wasn't talking to him, but to herself, as if she was alone. She lit another cigarette.

"There were arms and legs everywhere," she said. "But there were some good memories, too. One night, there were some soldiers who were brought in from various regiments who had been scrambled as they fought. And Zephyr was one of them."

"Zephyr," Percy said.

"We both almost broke into tears. All this time, we became so close just through writing letters to each other, and we were never physically close to each other, it felt like we had been in love for fifty years."

L, O, C, T, S, V went through Percy's mind.

Macy explained that Zephyr had multiple injuries, including two shots to the shoulder plus multiple gashes due to a blast from a tank. He had a head injury which had put him in such a stupor that he couldn't walk in a straight line.

"When I saw him being carried in, I had to make sure that I wasn't dreaming. I splashed water on my face and looked again, and he was there."

She flicked the ashes of her cigarette into her cup. She said that Zephyr had stayed at the recovery station for a week as his injuries healed. As much as he was happy to have a break from the war and to be taken care of by Macy, he was anxious to get back to Barlow and the gang to continue fighting. Macy could remember, word for word, certain conversations they had.

"I was completely immersed in love," she said. "The way he looked at me while he was all bandaged up—his eyes, they looked at me as if nothing else existed."

"Letters," Percy said.

Macy went on to say that the first time they kissed was while he was at the recovery station.

"It was two days before he had to leave."

Percy thought about Monica and how there were certain moments during their college days when they could've kissed each other. He wondered how or if this would have changed the dynamics of their relationship.

"Kiss," he said.

"His eyes were so watery," Macy said. "We both knew that the end was near, and he asked me to help him re-adjust his body because he was feeling uncomfortable."

She sighed.

"And when I leaned in to help him, our lips touched."

"I feel like kissing is great," Percy said.

"And we kissed for what seemed like an infinite amount of time, though it was only for a few seconds."

"Never-ending moments," Percy said.

"And to be honest, as we kissed, I didn't think I would see him again after he left the station. With the injuries he had sustained, in addition to going back to the war, I didn't think he would make it back home."

She spat into her tea cup.

"I think he believed it, too," Macy said. "It was the first time I was in love."

"What does love feel like?" Percy asked.

Macy looked into Percy's eyes for the first time. She smiled—one of the few smiles she had ever given to Percy.

"Oh Penelope," she said. "If you have to ask, I don't think I can explain it. You will know one day, and I hope to still be around so that you can explain it to me."

"Love love love love," Percy said.

He realized that Macy still hadn't talked about the tin cups. He pointed at them.

"But what about the purple tin cups?"

Macy fiddled with one of them. She said that after Zephyr left she became quite emotional—she couldn't focus and was constantly in tears, and one of the injured soldiers noticed.

"He asked me what was wrong, and I told him about Zephyr, and it turned out that they were actually in the same regiment. He told me that once he got back, that he'd look after him."

Percy looked at the tin cup in Macy's hands.

"He gave me these tin cups and said that once we all got back home from the war, Zephyr and I would be sitting together drinking out of these tin cups."

Macy explained that he had gotten them from a family whom he helped evacuate their house because of possible danger. It was a token of gratitude for they didn't have much.

"I didn't even know the soldier's name—he left that same day to go back to his regiment."

"Those are great cups," Percy said. "I like tin."

"Just knowing the meaning behind it—the history behind these items, so special. And it was then when I started coming up with the idea of — ."

Macy stopped talking in the middle of her sentence and cleared her throat. Percy expected her to finish what she was saying, but she abruptly changed the topic. She looked at the window.

"Looks like it might rain," Macy said.

She became silent, and Percy remained quiet, too as they looked through the window, waiting for the rain to come. Macy finally broke her trance and stood up, and as she walked away, she spoke.

"Enjoy your time off, Penelope, because when you get back to work, you won't have time to sneeze."

Percy went back to his apartment and saw that the red light on the answering machine was blinking. It was Monica. As soon as she said, "Hey Percy," he recognized her voice. She had found his phone number on the internet. She had moved back to Atlanta a few months ago. She had moved from San Diego, where she had gone after she graduated from college, working on her MBA. Percy played the message over a couple of times and wrote down her phone number. When he picked up the phone to call her, he couldn't push the numbers. There was some kind of force field between the phone dial and his fingertips.

He walked over to Macy's house to tell her that Monica had called, but she didn't answer the door when he knocked. He looked through the window and saw that the lights were on—worried that Macy may have been in trouble, perhaps she had fallen down, he opened the front door and walked in. He called her name out a few times, but no one answered. On the kitchen table, there were scraps of paper with initials and numbers on them. There was also a flashlight. He waited for a while for Macy to come back, but she never came. Dinner, he remembered. He went back to his apartment to take a nap and when he woke up, Barlow's car was back in the driveway—he walked back over to Macy's place to see how things were going. It took her a few minutes to open the door.

"How was your night?" Percy asked.

He followed Macy to the living room where Barlow sat.

"Hello there son," Barlow said.

"Call me Percy," he said.

Barlow took a sip from his glass. There was a pitcher of iced tea on the coffee table. Macy brought Percy a glass from the kitchen.

"Does Barlow know about the Wrights?"

"I had completely forgotten about that," she said.

Macy told Barlow about the news concerning the theft of Ted's vase. Barlow wasn't too sympathetic.

"If I remember correctly," Barlow said, "each one of us brought back something valuable from the War. I know Ted got his vase, but now I'm trying to remember what the rest of us brought back. I think Walter got an extremely old copy of the Torah. A father of a Jewish family gave Walter the book as a gift for their services and bravery."

"I remember now," Macy said. "Though the cover was almost falling apart, and some of the pages were coming out, it looked beautiful. Walter loved that gift. Didn't he devote much of his time to reading the Torah once he came back?"

Barlow nodded his head.

"What did Carl get?" Percy asked.

There were a few seconds of silence as Macy and Barlow thought about what Carl brought back from the War. Percy pretended to think though he had no clue as to what Carl could have brought back. He looked at Barlow and decided that he didn't like him. He didn't like the way he looked—he appeared deceptive and he looked mean. Barlow sat with this elbow resting on the table and his hand covering the lower portion of his face. Percy had a strange feeling that he was hiding something, and he didn't like that he had been visiting Macy all of a sudden, not out of jealousy, but more for the reason that he seemed shady.

"An umbrella?" Percy said.

"I remember now," Barlow said. "Pieces of brick and rubble from one of the houses that had been destroyed during the War. Carl had been rummaging through this house and found pictures of the family who had lived in the house. He felt horrible. He wanted to find them and free them if they were still alive. I don't think he ever did, though. But he came back with a few pictures and some bricks from that house. He didn't care about anything else he had."

Macy nodded her head and gazed into the ground. Percy started to think about Monica.

"So what was it that you and Zephyr brought back?" Percy asked.

"I didn't bring anything back," Barlow said. "I was just happy the whole thing was over with. My gift was being able to come back to America."

Barlow grunted.

"Do you remember what Zephyr brought back?" Macy asked. "I remember him mentioning something when he returned to America, but he never really explained what it was. In fact, I don't think I ever really knew what it was."

Barlow finished his drink and gazed into the carpet.

"I can't seem to remember, Macy," he said.

He looked around the living room. Percy stepped outside and sat on the porch, realizing that he should let Barlow and Macy spend some time together or that maybe he was intruding on their conversation. He thought about Monica. He was debating whether he should call her the next day or not. He told himself that he would decide in the morning—the thought of getting back in touch with Monica made him nervous, and not only getting back in touch with her, but the fact that she had moved back to Atlanta. Percy never thought that she would come back after leaving Georgia. Her family lived in California, and he assumed she would live closer to her parents. He went back to the apartment, not saying bye to Macy or Barlow.

Barlow didn't stay for too long. About a half-hour after Percy had gone back to the apartment, he looked out the window—Barlow's car was not in the driveway. He went back to Macy's house. She was sitting on the porch with a cigarette in hand. He looked at Macy's glass—it looked similar to the drink that Barlow had while sitting on the sofa.

"It's a little bit of gin."

"That's unusual," he said.

"Yes it is. But tonight is a good night to have it."

Percy poured himself a little bit.

"You don't like Barlow too much."

He thought that he had done a good job of hiding it.

"It's not so much that I don't like him," Percy said. "There's something eerie about him. It seems like he's hiding something."

"There is something about him I can't figure out," Macy said. "We've aged so much."

"He looked mean, too," Percy said. "I don't trust him."

Macy slowly nodded her head. He had never seen Macy in such a down mood before. He sipped the gin and wanted to spit it back out, but instead he gulped it down, trying hard not to make a face. He looked at Macy, who appeared to be in a daze.

"Are you okay?" Percy asked.

"Just a bit tired. Tired of it all."

"How was the dinner?"

"It was good," Macy said.

She quietly repeated the word "good" a few more times.

"It was good," she said again. "Grilled chicken and roasted potatoes."

"It can't be as good as your cooking, though," Percy said.

"Shut it, Penelope."

"Did Barlow say anything to put you off?" Percy asked.

"Tell me about your past, Penelope. I know nothing about you except for your allergies and inability to garden."

Percy sat back in his chair and slouched a bit to get comfortable. He took another sip of the gin and it went down smoother this time though he still made a face. Macy sat in the rocking chair across from him and gave him all of her attention. He told her how he didn't know who his parents were, and how he grew up in a shelter until he was eighteen.

"I ended up getting a scholarship for students coming from shelters and attended the University of Georgia."

"You already have such a history, and no one could ever know about it. It's all hidden in your head. It's astonishing how we keep these things inside us, and no one would ever know anything about them."

"It wasn't too bad," he said. "Nowadays, these shelters keep up to par."

"The intestines of our lives," Macy said.

"It really isn't a big deal anymore," Percy said. "I've made a few friends since then, during college, and of course, I met you. What more could I ask for?"

Macy laughed.

"A lot more," she said. "Especially when it comes to me, but I'm glad you were able to make some friends during college."

"Friends," Percy said.

"And here you are now. Working hard, and becoming an adult."

"Something like that," he said. "I have a long way to go. One day I would like to own my own business—a boudin specialty shop. And then maybe mix it in with other cuisines like boudin enchiladas or boudin and waffles. It'll be tough, but I think I can find a way to put boudin on the market here—the first time I had it was when I went to Louisiana."

"You can't even cook, Penelope," Macy said.

"Microwave," Percy said. "I also want to see Oprah."

He took one of Macy's cigarettes and lit it as he rocked back and forth in her chair. He coughed a few times.

"How do you do this?" Percy asked.

"I've been smoking since I was a teenager," Macy said. "It'll come to you—you'll get used to it. Though I don't condone it."

Percy took another drag and coughed again. He gave the rest of the cigarette to Macy.

"Barlow will drop by tomorrow," Macy said. "He's leaving his car here and he'll be taking a trip to South Carolina and Virginia. I guess he's looking for our other friends."

"When is he going?"

"I think in a couple of days," she said. "He'll be back in Atlanta. He's in good shape for his age. If I remember correctly, he's a year younger than me, but he seems ten years younger. He drove from Florida to here, which can be considered an achievement at his age. Good eyesight and no bent back. I wonder how he does it."

"You're not in too bad a shape yourself, Macy."

"Quit it, Penelope."

15

Percy called Monica the next morning. He caught her right before she was going to work. He was nervous.

They couldn't talk for too long, but she asked him to meet her at the Atlanta Stay Inn at 5:15 in the evening. That's where she worked. Percy had eight hours to back out.

He went to Macy's house. When she opened the door, she wore pink fluffy slippers, a red muumuu, and a white towel around her head.

"You look like a Valentine's Day advertisement," Percy said.

"You look like I'm going knock you down, Penelope," Macy said.

They sat on the porch.

"Are you enjoying your break?" Macy asked.

"I'm meeting an old friend in the evening."

"Looks like the past coming to the present for both of us."

"I'm kind of nervous."

"Zephyr used to be nervous when he was around me."

"How did it all happen anyway?" he asked. "I never got the rest of that story."

"When Zephyr came back after the War, it was like nothing had changed. We continued as friends.

We would spend hours together talking and having fun. It was such a great time, the actual beginning process of love."

Macy spat into the garden and lit a cigarette. Percy was amazed at the number of hidden pockets Macy had on her muumuu.

"One night, he and I went out for dinner," she said. "The rest of our friends had gone to the movie hall, but Zephyr wanted to take me out. And over dinner, he told me how he felt about me. It was funny though. The whole time he had a bit of spinach on his chin, and I didn't know how to tell him as he professed his feelings for me. I felt the same way about him, but I didn't immediately respond."

Percy fiddled with the sleeves of his shirt. The sweat on his brow dripped down to his chin. He noticed that his shoelaces were untied but didn't bother to fix them.

"Poor thing," Macy said. "He must have felt bad that night. But the next morning, when he knocked on my door, he stood there with some torn leaves on his chin and the biggest smile. He was making a joke out of what happened the night before. I laughed so hard, wiped his chin, and kissed him."

"I like spinach," Percy said.

"I think about it at least once every day," Macy said.

"Spinach and cheese," Percy said.

The Wrights Up The Reward Amount

In a recent statement, Leo Wright states that the reward is up to $14,000. If anyone knows the whereabouts of the vase, contact the police or him.*

"The house is lifeless without it," Leo says. "Every time I look at the mantle and see that it's not there, I feel like I'm not in my own home."

*Editor's Note: I wish I could get that vase back to them. $14,000! Do you know what you can do with that much money? I sure don't—never had that much saved up before, but I think I would throw a huge pizza party.

The article showed a picture of Leo and Jennifer at some kind of party or convention. Leo was holding up a glass of champagne—it looked like he was giving a toast of some sort.

Percy arrived at the hotel around 5 and sat in the lobby. He looked at a lady who was walking through the lobby. She wore a black business suit and was talking on a cellular phone. She stopped in the middle of the reception area and faced Percy. Monica. She was in the middle of a phone conversation. Percy didn't wave or make any gestures but watched her as she talked. She moved her free hand up and down, and she walked in circles in the middle of the lobby. She looked the same. Her black hair came down to her shoulders. It was longer than he remembered. She looked like she had also been tanning as her face was darker. He had never seen her that dark before. She was still fit—the bottom of her business skirt ended just above the middle of her calves, revealing the neatly compact muscles on her legs. She must have continued to run and exercise as she did during college, Percy thought. Monica laughed, talked for a few more seconds, and hung up the phone. She started looking around the lobby. That was Percy's cue.

"Monica."

She turned around and without saying anything, hugged him.

"It's so good to finally see you again."

"I'm fine and you?" he said.

Percy was so nervous that he didn't realize what Monica was saying—he just made up her words in his head and answered them out loud as if she had actually spoken those words to him. He tried hard to look into her eyes but was having a tough time doing so, as he kept looking away in an effort to ease his nervousness.

"I've been dying to see you since I got back to Georgia. But I wanted to be able to spend time with you rather than just talking for five minutes. And I finally have some time now, after I've settled down and everything."

"So you work here?"

He watched people coming in and out of the hotel lobby.

"I'm working as a marketing consultant. I love it. I just need to get used to the amount of time the job requires."

Percy was always a sucker for her brown eyes—he tried hard not to get lost in them when he finally managed to look at her.

"Let's get out of here," Monica said. "Are you hungry? I'm starved."

They sat in the sandwich shop—Monica was the same cheerful and lively person. Talking to her made Percy realize how much he had changed himself. He wasn't the joyful person that he was a few years ago during his college years with Bill and Monica. He felt like he was dragging the whole meeting down. He thought that he wasn't a fun guy anymore. Fun for Percy was sitting on the porch and drinking iced tea with Macy. After he told Monica about Macy, she was interested in meeting her. They exchanged addresses.

"Those days at the movie theater were so much fun," Monica said.

"I think about those times a good bit," Percy said. "I always think about when we would sneak in through the broken door late at night, and you would do cartwheels down the hallways."

"My favorite moment was when you were mopping the floor and you slipped and fell down, and as everyone stood and watched, you ended up doing some kind of mime performance or more like you were pretending to be Charlie Chaplin."

Percy had once told Monica that Charlie Chaplin was one of his favorite actors, and Percy smiled as Monica brought up that moment, realizing that she had remembered their late-night conversations about movies and actors.

"I wasn't acting," Percy said. "I really was trying to stand up, but I just couldn't."

Monica laughed at his confession.

"Those college days were fun," Percy said. "I think about those times quite often."

"I do, too." There was a pause. "And I'm glad I'm back," Monica said. "And I'm glad to reconnect with you."

Percy tried to speak, but only a series of incoherent words came out. He looked at his half-eaten turkey and cheese sandwich.

"This sandwich is pretty good," he said. "If I were to make a sandwich it would've been just like this one. I'm glad, too."

Monica took the last bite of her sandwich. The place barely had anyone in it, which Percy liked. He enjoyed empty restaurants, yet he loved to watch people in hotel lobbies and airports.

"Do you have a girlfriend?" Monica asked.

"I don't. I mean, you're a friend and a girl and so is Macy, but as far as girlfriends, I don't. I don't think I've ever had one."

"You should try it out," Monica said. "You will make someone really happy one day."

"Happy," Percy replied.

Monica looked at him and then at her watch.

"I actually have to head back to the hotel and finish up some work."

"I'll walk you back to the hotel then."

She insisted on paying for his dinner, and after a few minutes of arguing over the bill, she paid for the sandwiches. They left the shop and went back to the hotel. She gave him a hug and told him that she would call him soon to do something.

As Percy was leaving, he could see some kind of sparkle coming from the side. He turned around and saw someone who was sitting in a chair and was talking on the phone. The sparkle came from a man's watch. When he turned back to Monica, she was already on her cell phone, walking away. Percy looked back at the man and saw that it was Barlow. He sat and talked on the phone while he looked at a plant that was next to his chair. Percy hid behind one of the pillars. On a small table was a pamphlet about the hotel. He picked it up and pretended to look through it. Barlow stood up and continued to talk on the phone. He walked back and forth, until he finally sat down again, but in a different chair. A few minutes later, two other men joined him in the lobby. They were the same age as Barlow. One man was using a walking cane. Barlow shook the men's hands and they all took a seat. They all leaned forward with their faces only a couple of inches apart. It looked like a football huddle.

Macy was working in the garden as Percy walked over to see what she was up to.

"Would you like some help?" he asked.

"Penelope," Macy said.

"Penelope," Percy said.

She wiped her hands on her lime green muumuu and sat down in the grass.

"Have a seat," she said.

Percy sat down across from her and sneezed as Macy lit a cigarette.

"I've been thinking about the War a lot lately," she said.

"It was a pretty big war," Percy said.

"Right. It was a big war."

She ran her hands through the blades of grass, staring into the ground. Percy did the same as he continued to sneeze. Macy broke her own trance.

"I would have these nightmares while I was there. I would repeatedly dream that Zephyr would send me letters but that they were blank, no words and covered in blood."

"No letters," Percy said.

"One time I almost left my station to go see if I could find where Zephyr was located, but one of the other nurses talked me out of it."

She puffed her cigarette, holding a few blades of grass in her other hand. Percy thought about letters.

"Stamps," he said.

Macy went on to tell Percy more stories of the time Zephyr was in the recovery station. While he was sleeping in bed, Macy would sit by his side, making sure he was sleeping in peace. Whenever he would wake up in the morning, he always smiled and said, "The most beautiful way to wake up." Macy recalled the conversation.

"I hope all of this ends soon," she said. "And we all can go back home. When we get back, would you like to go out with me again? We can go dancing."

"You know I can't dance," Zephyr said. "But I will dance with you, and only with you."

Macy told Percy how she put her hand on Zephyr's forehead.

"You feel feverish," she said.

"Remember when we used to play hopscotch and skip rope when we were younger, and I had hurt my ankle?"

"I vaguely remember," Macy said.

"We were on the sidewalk, and I was shouting in pain, you put your hand on my forehead to see if I had a fever."

Macy explained to Percy that as they were having this conversation, the shrill sounds of war could be heard in the background but neither of them gave any attention to the loud clashes.

"I wish we were playing hopscotch and jumping rope," Zephyr said.

Macy put the palm of her hand against Zephyr's face as the ground shook from the war.

"Or I wish we were just dancing," Zephyr said.

"I'll lead," Macy said.

Macy finished her story and went back into a daze. Percy looked at her hands as they grazed the grass, making a soft sound.

"I miss him," Percy said.

"I do too," Macy said.

She put out her cigarette and spat. Percy spat as well and they continued to work in the garden.

17

M.M.C.

Terms Of Agreement

Addendum 2 (Attire):

Only colorful muumuus shall be worn—bright colors—Oranges, Greens, Blues, and Yellows, and such. If your muumuu darkens the room, you shall be asked to leave or change into another muumuu. Please, with color comes fun.

No sunglasses unless you have provided a note from your physician specifying eye-related matters and problems.

18

Percy had two days until he started working for Macy again. He hadn't talked to Monica since he had met her at the hotel, nor had he seen Barlow since he had seen him talking to the two guys in the lobby of the same hotel.

The phone rang and he picked up thinking that it was Monica.

"It's Allen."

He mumbled, sounding drunk. Percy heard a lot of clutter in the background and only bits and pieces of his sentences. Percy told him that he would talk to him later when he was in a better state of mind to have a conversation and hung up. He went over to Macy's house and knocked on the door a couple of times, but she didn't answer. He twisted the knob—the door wasn't locked. He called her name, but there was no response. He listened hard to hear if the shower was on, or if she was in the bathroom, but he didn't hear anything. The kitchen and living room were tidy. He walked through the hallway to her bedroom. He knocked lightly on the bedroom door, but there was no response. He shut her door and went to the kitchen to make a turkey sandwich. A few bites into it, he heard the sound of a car engine in the driveway—there was a green Buick LeSabre in the driveway. There was a man in the driver's seat, and another man was sitting in the passenger seat. They waved to Percy, backed out of the driveway, and drove away.

When Macy came back home later that day, Percy was already there, sitting on the porch. Macy looked worn out, and her clothes were creased.

"I'm starving," she said. "And exhausted."

Percy asked her what she had been up to, and Macy said that she had been running errands all day.

"Want me to make you a sandwich?" Percy asked.

"I'm fine. I'm almost too tired to even eat."

She sat on the porch and took out a cigarette.

"I'm getting too old for this, Penelope."

"Too old for what?" Percy asked.

"Just too old."

"I think you're doing just fine."

Percy told Macy about this episode later on that day. She had gone out with Barlow to an antique store. She wasn't surprised about the Buick.

"So many people drive by looking for a certain house and they get lost. I've had to give a few directions to strangers who have driven up onto the driveway."

"Barlow didn't go on his trip yet?" Percy asked.

"He decided to stay a bit longer in Atlanta and spend time with me. It's nice to be talking to him on a regular basis again."

"Do you like him?" Percy asked.

"Not like that, Penelope. There's only one guy in my life now."

As much as Macy had picked on Percy, it was those statements that made him feel loved. She asked Percy if he had talked to his friend yet.

"She wants to meet you," Percy said.

"Maybe we could all have dinner one night."

"I can cook," Percy said.

"No you can't," Macy replied.

"No I can't."

He rocked back and forth in his chair.

19

"May I take you out?" Percy asked.

They were sitting on the porch—it had been raining all day, but it was finally letting up as it turned into a drizzle. Percy noticed that Macy looked bored as she sat in the rocking chair, smoking a cigarette and sipping gin as she stared at the wooden floorboards. She didn't hear Percy's question. He asked her again which took Macy out of her daze.

"What's that?" Macy replied.

"Would you like to get some dinner tonight?"

"Have a seat, Penelope."

Percy looked around. He was already sitting, but he stood up and sat back down. From the pocket of her muumuu, she pulled out a piece of paper and gave it to Percy.

My Dear M,

It's a pretty day, and I, of course, thought about you, and here I am writing this letter. The troops look down today, despite the nice weather. No one is talking, they all sit quietly, waiting for orders. No laughing, no shooting, no games, nothing. I understand their sentiments, but I must find ways to be hopeful, to be happy, and the only way I can do this is by thinking of you and writing to you. I'm lying down with my head against my backpack, staring at the sky. The clouds are moving fast, and I hope we move along just as fast—to be home—and to ask you out again, but this time, my teeth will be clean of spinach. I will write to you again, on another pretty day.

Fondly,
Z

"Oh, letters," Percy said.

He felt like he should cry, but he couldn't get any tears to come out. He scrunched his face and bit his tongue, but still, no tears. He could tell that Macy was feeling emotional, and he was trying to match her feelings.

"This is pretty," Percy said.

"And there are several more letters," Macy said. "I have them all. The rain made me think about this particular letter."

"Letters," Percy said.

"I haven't looked at them since Zephyr's funeral. It has been quite some time now."

"You seem sad," Percy said. "I would like to take you out for dinner."

"Sometimes it's good to be sad. Or bad or mad. Otherwise, we would all be numb. Never be numb, Penelope."

"I've felt bad before," Percy said.

Macy sipped the last of her gin before spitting it out into the garden. She lit another cigarette. Percy noticed that her hands were shaking.

"I don't think I could even imagine you feeling any kind of madness or sadness to be honest. Tell me about it."

"Like now?"

"Like now."

"I feel sad right now," Percy said.

"Why?"

"Because you seem sad. I am sad when you are sad."

"Quit it, Penelope," Macy said. "What about another time?"

"One time I cried," Percy said.

He tried to tear up again, but nothing came out.

"It was during my first year of college, during Thanksgiving break. My friends were with their families so I just drove around for a bit at night looking for a place to eat."

He thought about the 24-hour diner which he still frequented. It was a lifesaver for him as it was open every day, including all holidays.

"As I drove around," Percy continued, "I kept seeing homeless people. One after another, sitting against buildings or on benches, covered in newspapers or garbage bags."

Percy sighed and asked for a cigarette. Macy gave him one, and he tried to light it with the butt of the cigarette sticking out.

"Turn it around," Macy said.

Percy flipped it around and lit it. He coughed to where tears started coming out, and his eyes became red.

"And just as I was starting to feel bad for myself, I realized that I didn't have it that bad at all. And after seeing one more homeless lady, I couldn't take it anymore and started to cry."

"That's understandable," Macy said. "After all, you are a thoughtful and caring person."

"So I went to the 24-hour diner and used all the money I had on me to buy food and gave it to as many homeless people as I could."

"Now that sounds like a great Thanksgiving," Macy said.

"I wonder how they're doing."

"Well, maybe another time, you can read more of these letters exchanged between Zephyr and me."

They both looked out of the patio, onto the street and beyond, in a daze, and they sat there quietly until the drizzling rain had fully stopped.

20

Dear Z,

I hope this letter finds you well. I'm glad that you are able to enjoy the pretty days—any kind of happiness in your situation must be so valuable. I think about you often. And by often, I mean all of the time. If I had known that you were enlisting during our time together in Atlanta, I would have surely given you more attention. I didn't do so, because I was trying to gain your attention by "not caring," if that makes sense.

You are a sweetheart.

I find myself to be so sad here, so much. Seeing wounded soldier after soldier, crying, screaming, praying, asking for their mothers—I am at a loss. But what keeps me going is doing my job, which is to help them to heal.

I think about home quite often, and I have an idea, a possible way to help others. It will be a business of some sort, but it won't be a popular one. I, of course, will explain it to you once we all go back to Atlanta.

Continue to fight every day, Z. By fighting, I don't necessarily mean fighting the war, but fighting for your spirit, your soul, your happiness.

Spinach forever, my dear.

—M

Dear M,

I must keep this short as we're about to move, but I just wanted to thank you for your letters—they keep me going. I want to say I love you, but I don't know how you would react. But I want to say it, just in case I don't come out of this alive.

I love you.

We're about to move north, but we don't know why yet. The gang is restless—they're ready for action. In one way or another, they want this all to end.

I've made several close friends—some are still alive, some I've watched die in my arms. I hope to make it back and hold you in my arms.

As Ever,
Z

My Dear Z,

I love you. I'm hearing good news about the war. We will be home soon, and I will be in your arms.

Love,
M

21

Percy knocked on Macy's door. He wore gray slacks and a button-up, long-sleeved dark blue shirt. He held a tie in one hand and flowers in the other. He had pulled them from Macy's garden—a collection of marigolds and roses. He loved the variety of colors—yellows, oranges, purples, and reds.

Macy opened the door—Percy was in awe of how she looked. She wore a long dark green gown and her hair was fixed in a complicated fashion. It was also the first time Percy saw her using cosmetics—though it was minimal—lipstick, a slight blush, and a tint of eyeliner. Percy was surprised.

"Penelope," Macy said.

"Good morning."

"It's evening."

"Hi evening," Percy said.

"You look nice, Penelope."

"You look like a chandelier."

Macy smiled. She opened her mouth to speak, but nothing came out. Percy tapped his foot to a song he was making up in his head. He realized that he should talk.

He held out the flowers.

"These are for you. I got them from the front garden."

He pointed to the area just in front of the patio. Macy looked at the flowers and then up at the evening sun.

"Thank you," she said. "They're lovely."

"Thank you," Percy said.

"I can't believe this still fits," she said.

"Oh, the slacks are pretty new. I got them a few months ago—I think I stopped growing for the most part."

"I once wore this dress on a date with Zephyr. I feel like an antique."

Percy jumped. "A valuable one," he said.

"Shut up, Penelope."

He asked her if she was ready for dinner.

"Famished," Macy said. "Where are we going?"

"It's a surprise," Percy said. "I've yet to go, but I hear that it's great."

"I'm sure it'll be fine."

As they approached the restaurant, Percy told Macy to close her eyes, and she acted accordingly. He parked and spoke with excitement.

"Open them," he said.

There was a red building in front of them with a huge sign at the top, reading "Popeyes."

Macy laughed.

"It's called Popeyes," Percy said. "They're supposed to have really good fried chicken. Have you ever been?"

"I hear it's good," Macy said.

"It has nothing do with the cartoon character, though. At least I don't think it does."

He got out of the car and rushed over to the other side to open the door for Macy.

"You're an old breed," she said.

She got out of the car and spat. Percy spat, too.

"Before we go in," he said. "Can you help me?"

He held out his tie. Without speaking, Macy gently took the tie from his hand and fixed it around Percy's neck.

"There you go," she said. "Dapper. You're giving me all kinds of flashbacks, Penelope."

They walked into Popeyes—no one else was inside, just them and the employees.

"How about a seat next to the window?" Percy asked.

"Sure," Macy said. "But I think we go to the counter and order first, and then we sit down."

"No waiter?"

"I don't think so."

They went to the counter. Percy stepped aside so Macy could order first—a three piece with a side of red beans and rice and a biscuit. Percy ordered the same, and they got their drinks at the fountain machine before sitting at the back of the restaurant, next to a window.

"This place smells so good," Percy said. "I can't wait to try the food. Popeyes."

Macy pulled out a flask from her purse and poured its content into her cup.

"Adds a little spice to the drink," she said.

Percy's eyebrows arched, his eyes widened.

"Oh wait. I'll be right back."

He darted outside and came back moments later with a candle inside a glass container. Macy had picked up their orders while he was at the car.

"Do you have a light?"

Macy pulled out a lighter, and Percy lit the candle, putting it in the middle of the table as they sat across from each other. One of the employees came over and said that due to fire safety regulations, the candle needed to be extinguished.

"Honey," Macy said. "I promise I'll put out any fire, and we'll take full responsibility for any damages."

"Damages," Percy said.

The employee smiled and was cordial, saying that it was okay.

"As long as there aren't any other customers in here," the employee said.

"Popeyes," Percy said.

The employee walked away, telling them to enjoy their meal. Macy turned her attention toward Percy.

"Well this is very sweet," she said.

Percy was excited.

"Let's eat and see," he said. "I've heard a lot of good reviews about this place. It's called Popeyes. I think it's a chain restaurant, too."

He waited for Macy to take the first bite. She picked up a drumstick and bit into it. He looked at her with anticipation.

"Lovely," she said. "Please eat."

Percy engulfed his first piece of fried chicken, closing his eyes and sighing with every bite.

"This is good chicken," he said. "And the red beans and rice is superb."

"Sure is. You know, I make a pretty good fried chicken, too."

"I'll have to try it," Percy said.

His voice was full of excitement.

"One day, Penelope."

She finished chewing.

"When we were in France during the war, there wasn't a day I didn't think about Zephyr."

"Zephyr," Percy said.

His mouth was full of fried chicken.

"It really is funny. I never really had any feelings for him while we were in Atlanta, nothing that amounted to any kind of love and affection. It's those letters that really won me over. Through our distance, we become close."

Percy bit into his biscuit.

"I like letters," he said.

"He was sentimental and strong. And then when I had to take care of him, I was determined to make it through the war with him to live together when we got back home."

Percy peeled the skin off a chicken breast and ate it.

"As you know me now," she said. "I was once quite a different person."

Percy could tell that Macy was feeling somewhat sad as she talked about Zephyr and the war, which in turn made Percy sad. His eyes became wide again.

"Oh wait," he said. "I'll be right back."

He ran to his car again, and when he came back, he held a small boombox. He put it on the table, next to the candle, and pressed play. Jazz music started to fill Popeyes. He held out his hand.

"Can I have this dance?" he asked.

Macy wiped her chin with her napkin and took a sip of her drink.

"How can I resist," she replied.

She took his hand, and Percy guided her to the middle of the restaurant.

"This is Coltrane," he said. "'A Few Of My Favorite Things.'"

"Love it."

"I don't know how to dance," Percy said. "I've never danced before."

"You'll get it, Penelope."

She guided his hands to where they needed to be. Then she took control, telling Percy where to move his feet.

"I can't remember the last time I danced," Macy said.

"Me either," Percy said.

"I know it was with Zephyr. That's right—it was shortly before his death."

She continued to guide Percy as they danced in the middle of Popeyes. The employees behind the counter looked at them, smiling. Macy spoke in a low tone.

"We were at a soiree, and we were both horribly bored as we sat and listened to people talk about nonsense."

Percy stared at his own feet, trying his best not to step on Macy, or to not stumble over her.

"And there wasn't any music playing," she said. "But Zephyr took my hand and we walked to the middle of the room and started to dance. Everyone was staring at us."

"Popeyes," Percy said.

"But we didn't care at all. We just twirled around the room listening to the music in our heads."

They continued to dance until the song ended.

"That was lovely," Macy said.

Percy was breathing hard, not used to moving around so much. He took her hand, and they walked back to their table, where he continued to eat his food. Macy sighed, before taking a sip of her drink.

"Thanks," she said.

"The fried chicken is so good," Percy said.

"For all of this. This was lovely."

"I love the red beans and rice," Percy said.

"I'll make you some fried chicken one day."

"And red beans and rice?"

"And red beans and rice."

After dinner, Percy took Macy back to her house. Macy was quiet the whole time, and Percy couldn't tell if she was sad or tired or just thinking. Percy helped Macy out of the car.

"Are you okay?" he asked.

"I am. I know I was quiet. I was just appreciating the night. Thanks again, Penelope."

After walking her to the door, he went back to his apartment and took a nap. When he woke up, he thought about his dream. He was a soldier, stationed in France during WWII, in the same regiment as Zephyr. He dreamt that they were close, looking after each other. He dreamt that he was there when Zephyr was hurt, and he was wrapping his wounds while listening to him talk about how he was falling in love with Macy, hoping to see her again.

"You'll see her," Percy said. "And you two will get married."

"You think so, P?" Zephyr asked. "You really think so?"

Zephyr's eyes were glossy, and he was breathing hard. The sounds of war created a bubble around them.

"I promise," Percy said.

He picked Zephyr up and positioned him over his shoulder and jogged away from immediate danger, putting him down behind a barrier they had made.

"I got to get back," Percy said.

"Stay," Zephyr said. "Tell me what's real."

"Macy is real. You're real. And your love for each other is real."

"You think?"

"I promise."

Percy patted him on the shoulder and ran back into a blurry vision of war.

Percy sat at the edge of his bed and tried to think about the rest of his dream. He rubbed his feet against the carpet and closed his eyes. He saw himself injured, in a makeshift hospital in France. Macy was taking care of him.

"Do you know Zephyr?" Percy asked.

Macy paused and took a deep breath.

"I do. Why?"

"He loves you."

"I love him."

"Have you ever been to Popeyes?" Percy asked.

"I've never heard of it," Macy said.

22

Early the next morning, around two, Percy heard noises outside the apartment. Allen was stumbling on the sidewalk. He had knocked over Macy's trashcan. By the time Percy had dressed and gone outside, Allen had knocked over the mailbox. He stood on the sidewalk and looked left then right to see if any cars were coming. He did this about five times. Percy went to see if Allen was in trouble, but he realized that he wasn't in trouble, just drunk.

"What are you doing here?" Percy asked.

Percy could smell the alcohol in his breath, and his eyes were barely open. In the distance, a dog was barking.

"Percy, it's me, Percy," Allen said. "It's Allen, Percy."

Percy picked up the trashcans and put the trash bags back into them. He fixed the mailbox.

"I know it's you. Are you okay? You're making a lot of commotion."

"I just wanted to talk, Percy. I've got no one to talk to, Percy. Joe won't talk to me anymore, Percy. Joe won't talk to me anymore."

"Did you drive here?" Percy asked.

"I almost killed myself."

"Who's Joe?"

Percy told him to come inside and get some sleep, and that he should drive back in the morning. Allen followed him into the apartment and sat on the floor.

"Don't you want to talk?" Allen asked.

A few seconds later he was sleeping. Percy went back to his bed. He remembered Joe—he was the waiter at the Lebanese restaurant—and made the connection that they must have been in a relationship together and had broken up.

When Percy woke up Sunday morning, Allen was in the kitchen making coffee. Percy didn't have any at the apartment, so Allen had gone out and bought some. Percy didn't have a percolator either, so he bought one of those as well.

"You need to go. Finish your coffee and leave."

"You're mad," Allen said. "I totally understand. I'm sorry—I just needed to be around someone I know last night."

"I'm not mad," Percy replied. "But the night is over now, and you've sobered up. Go get some food."

"I don't know what happened between us," Allen said. "We were doing great, and then before we knew it, we had broken up, hating each other."

Percy became more sympathetic toward Allen. He could tell he was really hurting.

"Maybe go talk to him," he said. "I'm not the best person to give relationship advice, but I hear talking is a big help."

Allen nodded his head.

"I just need to hear someone tell me that. Thanks. I'll make this coffee to-go."

"But that's my mug," Percy said.

Allen looked at the mug he held in his hand.

"It's a nice mug," he said.

"Keep it. And take your percolator as well."

He took Percy's mug but left the coffee percolator in the kitchen. Percy went over to Macy's house around noon. She was sitting on the porch when he arrived, smoking a cigarette and drinking iced tea.

"I need to buy some items for dinner tomorrow," she said. "If I make you a list, could you get the groceries? I go to the one just down the block from here. I'll make you some fried chicken another day, but for tomorrow, I'm thinking of country fried ham with gravy, and vegetables and biscuits. Maybe some mashed potatoes, too."

Percy nodded, and she wrote out a list for him. She offered Percy the money for the groceries, but he refused.

"Even though you're cooking, I'm treating you to dinner," he said.

"Again," she said.

Macy patted him on the back.

"You're quite the gentleman," she said. "And thanks again for dinner the other day. I had a lovely time, Percy."

"Percy," he said.

It took him about an hour to get all the things she needed, and when he got back, Macy wasn't home anymore. He unpacked the groceries and put them in the fridge or in the cupboard. As he walked outside to get the remaining bags from the car, he saw the same Buick LeSabre he had seen the other day driving by. The driver looked at Percy. This time, the man didn't wave but sped off. Percy ran to his car, backed out in a hurry, and sped down the street. The Buick was not too far off. Percy slouched a bit in the seat to make it harder for the driver to recognize him. The Buick crossed the intersection and took a right into a Walgreen's parking lot. Percy pulled in as well and parked two rows behind the Buick. It had a South Carolina license plate. He could see another man in the passenger seat. They didn't get out of the Buick but sat inside with the engine still running. Percy got out of his car. They didn't notice him until he knocked on the window of the driver. The two men stopped talking and looked at him. The driver locked the car doors and lowered his window about an inch from the top.

"Can I help you?" Percy asked.

"Excuse me?" the driver said.

"I've seen you twice outside the house on Euclid Avenue. Can I help you?"

"No we're fine," the driver said. "We got lost."

"Twice, at the same spot? Where are you trying to go? Maybe I can help you find it."

He heard the man in the passenger seat mumble something to the driver. The driver put his window all the way down. The other man pulled out a walking cane, grunted, and hit Percy in the stomach with the wooden stick, causing him to kneel on the ground, gasping for breath as the driver backed out and sped away.

When Percy returned to the apartment, Barlow's car was in the driveway. He didn't feel like dealing with him and went to the apartment, waiting for Macy to be by herself so he could tell her about the incident with the Buick.

Again, he woke up to a loud noise coming from outside. It sounded like glass was being broken, or something was being thrown to the ground. Percy thought that Allen was prowling outside again. It was around one in the morning. He still felt an acute pain in his stomach whenever he twisted his body. He stretched it out a bit, but the hurting didn't go away. He looked outside and saw the Buick parked in Macy's driveway. He ran to Macy's house, not bothering to put on his shoes.

He twisted the knob, but the door was locked. This was only the second time that Percy had tried to walk in and found that the door had been locked. He placed his ear to the door and heard shuffling and movement in the house. He ran to Macy's garage and got the toolbox. It didn't take too long for the knob to come off. But the door didn't budge. Percy looked through the doorknob hole and he saw a light in the living room. Some of Macy's antiques were on the floor. They were broken. A man walked across the hallway. He wore a ski cap and was dressed in black. Another man was carrying Macy's body across the hallway to the living room. She wasn't screaming or struggling.

Percy kicked the door several times.

"Shoes," he said.

After a few attempts, the door pushed inwards. When he walked in, he saw three men standing in the hallway. All of them were in black and their faces were masked.

"The police are on the way," he shouted.

The three men looked at each other but didn't say anything.

"Where is Macy?"

Percy took a few steps forward. One man held a walking cane. Percy rubbed his own stomach. Another man was holding a lamp in his hand, and the other held a bag that was half full. He had a sparkling gold watch around his wrist. Barlow. Percy went after him first.

"I knew it," Percy said.

Once Percy was in hitting distance, the man with the cane swung at him. Following him, the other man tried to hit Percy with the lamp. Percy stepped back before they could make any contact. He felt the cuts on the bottom of his feet from stepping on small pieces of broken glass. The blood smudged against the wooden floor of the entrance hallway. The man with the lamp swung again, and as he missed Percy stepped forward and hit Barlow in the face. It was the first time Percy had ever hit someone. Even as a child, when the other kids would pick on him at the shelter, Percy never fought back. Barlow fell straight to the floor. The man with the lamp and the man with the walking cane hit Percy in the back. Percy turned around and grabbed the walking cane from the man and threw it on the floor. He saw the lamp swinging again and moved out of the way just in time. Percy was able to quickly glance at Macy in the living room—her eyes were closed and she was motionless. He punched the man with the lamp and he fell to the floor. And as he was about to hit the last man standing, he could just see with the corner of his eyes Barlow coming. Percy fell to the floor.

23

House Broken Into: One Dead And One Hospitalized

Late last night, Macy Thorpewaite's house was broken into. Her house was wrecked as many of her belongings were shattered and broken. Macy was announced dead at the scene. However, there were no signs of blood or bruises or any kind of physical fight. Early this morning it was announced that she had died of a heart attack.

Also found in the house was Macy's neighbor, Percy Winks. He was on the floor with blood coming from the back of his head. His stomach was bruised. He has been hospitalized and he should be able to fully recover.

No one has been linked to the crime as of yet.

More information as it comes to us.

24

He heard a buzzing noise. He turned around to get more comfortable, but he felt something stuck to his wrist that kept him from turning. This made him open his eyes. He saw the ceiling lights—long tubes which made the buzzing sound. A blanket covered his body. He felt nauseous and thirsty. It took him a few minutes to realize that he had woken up in a hospital room. He turned his head and couldn't see anyone else in the room. The television mounted on the wall was playing Oprah. Four o'clock, he thought. He liked her show. He liked the way she held herself on television, and he liked the issues she covered. She did a lot for people. She gave back to people. He would always think that if he ever got a large amount of money, he would give it to charity, especially to shelters for children without parents.

It took Percy another few minutes to remember what had happened the night before at Macy's house. He saw the I.V. attached to his right hand. He wasn't too good at being around needles, so he tried not to look at it anymore. Where was Macy? Did those men escape? If they did, Percy vowed, while lying in the hospital bed, that he would get them. Why would they do such a thing to Macy? Especially Barlow. Even though he didn't like him, he would never expect him to harm Macy, nor steal anything from her.

A nurse walked into the room. She asked Percy how he was feeling. He mumbled something in reply, and she did something with the I.V. She checked his blood pressure and told him there was a pitcher of water and a glass next to the bed. His eyelids felt heavy—just a little more sleep, and then maybe later he could figure out what had happened.

When he woke up again, a numbness at the back of his head had replaced the pain. He was angry that he wasn't able to handle the three guys. He thought they were too old to fight properly, and he also thought that he was doing pretty well until he fell to the ground. The television set was off. Percy felt dampness on the bed sheets. He pushed the button to call for the nurse.

"Let me get it for you, Percy," Allen said.

Allen was sitting in a chair beside him.

"How are you feeling?" Allen asked.

"How long have you been here?"

"A couple of hours."

"How come you're here?" Percy asked.

"It's been a hectic night for you, Percy. I'll explain things to you when you're a little bit better."

Percy was glad that Allen was in the room with him. He never thought that it would happen, but he was happy to see him. Allen poured a glass of water for him, placed it right before his lips, and tilted his head forwards so that Percy could sip it.

"I need new bed sheets."

"I'll get the nurse—be right back."

Percy laid his head back to the pillow and closed his eyes again, not to sleep, but to situate everything again. He hoped that Macy was in the next room also recovering from last night and that by tomorrow, they would be on her porch drinking iced tea and having a good time.

Allen came back followed by a nurse. She held a new set of bed sheets in her hand.

"Let me help you up so that the nurse can change the sheets," Allen said.

He held his arm with one hand, and held the I.V. stand with the other and guided Percy out of bed.

"Since you're up, do you need to use the restroom?" he asked.

Percy nodded.

"Need my help, or do you think you can manage?"

Percy told him that he would try on his own. When he returned to the room, the bed was made. The nurse said she would be back with the doctor shortly. Percy got back into bed, and Allen pulled a chair up next to him.

"How're you feeling champ?" he asked.

"What happened?"

"Well, I'm not sure what you remember and what you have forgotten, but I'll tell you what happened when I arrived. But the important thing is to remain relaxed. The more you stay relaxed, the faster the recovery will be."

He explained to Percy that he had dropped by the apartment late last night in a drunken state as he had done before. He knocked on the door for a few minutes and then decided to leave. He walked down the steps that led up to the apartment and was walking past Macy's house when he stumbled and tripped over a hard object. As he was getting up, he noticed Macy's door was open, and a flickering light coming from somewhere inside. He picked up the object that he had tripped on. It was an antique clock. Allen walked into Macy's house and saw Percy lying facedown on the ground with broken pieces of decorative objects everywhere.

The flickering lamplight was coming from the living room. There, he saw Macy, also lying facedown on the floor.

"It sobered me up in a second," Allen said. "And here we are now."

"How's Macy?" Percy asked.

Allen looked at the floor and then to the window directly across from him.

"I'm sorry, but Macy is dead."

Percy could feel the tears getting ready to form, but nothing came out. He wanted to scream, but he couldn't open his mouth.

"She was pronounced dead at the scene," Allen said. "She had a heart attack."

"Heart attack?"

Percy pictured Macy's face. He needed to remember a clear visual image of her face. He remembered the last words she spoke to him. He wanted to cry, but the tears didn't come out. He couldn't remember the last time he cried, maybe when Monica left Atlanta, he thought. The doctor and the nurse came in.

Doctor Bralin told Percy that he had a concussion and that he became unconscious after he was hit on the back of the head. The skin had split open, and this had caused him to lose a great deal of blood. He had thirty stitches keeping the skin on the back of his head together. As he touched the top of his head, he realized that his hair was shaved closely down to the skin. He was to take antibiotics, rub a special cream on the wound, drink water, and get rest. The doctor summed up the situation saying that he was extremely lucky because it could have been a lot more serious.

Allen had to go back to the university because some classes had already finished their final projects, and he needed to be there to supervise and evaluate them. He left his cell phone number next to the telephone and told Percy that he would be able to take him back home whenever he was released.

Percy thought about the three men. It looked like they were looking for something. They had been going through all her things and breaking things during their search. Did Macy have a heart attack because the men were breaking into her house? Or did she already have the heart attack? What could they want to steal from Macy, except for antiques and good food? As he was staring at the ceiling, Monica walked in holding a plant.

"I got this for you," she said.

"I'm lost," Percy said.

"Don't worry," Monica said. "I'm here. You'll be okay."

"How did you know I was here?"

She placed the plant next to the window.

"It was in the news. How are you?"

"How are you?"

She laughed.

"I'm sorry about all of this," she said.

Dr. Bralin entered the room followed by a nurse—he told Percy that he could go home, but that he needed to rest. Percy signed the release forms and Monica took him back to the apartment. Percy called Allen and told him that someone was taking him back and that he would talk to him later. Monica and Percy didn't talk much during the drive back home. He glanced at Macy's house as Monica pulled up to the apartment. She couldn't pull into the driveway because it was marked off with yellow tape. Monica helped him walk up the stairs to the apartment, but she couldn't stay long—she had to go back to work.

Percy sat on his bed and looked around his room—it was all a blur to him, and his way back to reality came in the form of remembering when he was living in the shelter for children. He remembered Mrs. Worthwise, one of the women who worked there and how she was sweet and kind. She always spoke to him like he was a puppy, and he would always listen to her and seek her advice as he became older. Before Macy, Mrs. Worthwise was the only other lady he had gotten close to, and now that both of them were out of his lives, he felt he was part of a brand new world, just as he had felt when he left the shelter when he turned eighteen—alone, clueless, and confused.

"Macy," he said.

"Please let me know if you find anything new," Percy said.

He was on his way out of the police station. The officer asked him a few questions about his whereabouts, and if he knew anyone that had any kind of malice toward Macy. Percy told them that he didn't know much, but that he had heard some crashing noises coming from her house, and that when he got there, he saw that three men, dressed in black, were looking for something. He also mentioned the Buick LeSabre that had been driving by the past few days. He didn't talk about Barlow and his friends, though, because Percy wanted to get to them first. He gave them information, but not enough information for them to find any leads. Percy wanted to take control of confronting the three men.

From the station, Percy went back to Macy's house—he had never seen the house in such a deserted state before. The remaining antiques had lost their zest. They didn't seem like they should belong in the house anymore—they were lifeless. The place used to be full of colors and history and things that clink and clank; now it was full of pieces of Macy's life strewn about the house. On the kitchen counter was a jar of tea. Percy washed a glass and made some iced tea using the light from the open refrigerator. He went outside on the porch, found one of Macy's cigarettes, and sipped his drink. He coughed, still having problems with how to smoke properly. He thought about the time when Macy showed him the model ship that Zephyr had made. Her eyes were so wide; her smile was so big. He took the last puffs of his cigarette and went back into the house. The ship was still in the china cabinet. Most of the things around it, plates, teacups, and vases were broken, but the model looked untouched. Did they know not to touch Macy's most prized possession? Did they forget to look in the china cabinet? Percy looked at the ship and marveled at its detailed creation. He wished he could have met Zephyr, and wondered if all of this would have happened if he was still around.

26

The hubbub in the Atlanta Stay Inn lobby was the most Percy had heard in a hotel. He didn't get much sleep—about four hours' worth—and he had forgotten to take his medicine. The pain was still in the back of his head, and his ribs were sore. He sat in a green chair at one of the corners of the lobby and waited to see if Barlow would walk through. He didn't watch random people this time but specifically kept looking at the lobby entrance from both the street-side and the hallway-side. His right leg was shaking up and down. He didn't want to look for Monica, either. He wanted Barlow.

There he was. He stood in the middle of the lobby with his sparkling gold watch. After a few minutes, he sat down on a chair and started to talk on his cell phone. Percy walked up to him and stood directly behind Barlow's chair, so he couldn't see him. He didn't realize exactly what he was doing, but he pulled the chair backward, causing him to fall over. There was a loud noise. Barlow stood up, trying to figure out what happened. He saw Percy and picked up the chair.

"You killed Macy," Percy said.

Barlow grabbed his cell phone.

"I thought you were dead, son," he said.

He almost whispered when he talked.

"Not your son," Percy said.

Barlow mumbled something on the phone.

"There were three of you," Percy said. "One against three?"

He hung up the phone and rubbed his temples, before looking around the lobby to see if anyone else was watching them.

"She was already dead when we got there," Barlow said.

"What were you looking for?"

"Did you tell the police?" Barlow asked.

Half of a key was sticking out of his pocket. The tag on the keychain read 202.

"How about I let you in on a secret?" Barlow said.

Percy noticed two shadows to the side of him. One man had a walking cane. Percy clenched his fists.

"Relax," Barlow said. "We're going to figure something out. No more violence."

"You all were the ones to start the violence. Not me or Macy. So yes, more violence."

This was the most aggressive and confident Percy had ever been. Though he was always picked on, both physically and emotionally, he had never fought back. This time was different. Percy kicked the walking cane out of the man's hand. The man took a couple of steps, bent down with a groan, and before he could pick it up, Percy kicked the walking stick away from him.

"That's just the start of it," Percy said.

As he lifted his right arm to strike, he felt a tap on his shoulder. A man dressed in a gray suit stood before him. He had a nametag that read: Jim Bern. He was one of the managers of the hotel. His stern face let Percy know that he had been watching them.

"Is there something wrong here, gentlemen?" Jim asked.

"These men broke into my neighbor's house and maybe killed my neighbor. Her name was Macy Thorpewaite."

Barlow and the two other men laughed, and Jim Bern laughed as well.

"I'm not joking," Percy said.

"Is everything okay?"

Percy recognized the tone—Monica.

"You shouldn't be here, Percy. With your head injury and all."

He looked at the hotel manager. He looked at the three men and nodded as if he just understood something.

"Head injury," Jim said. "I see. Is there someone I should call? Doctor? Therapist?"

"I'm not crazy," Percy said.

"I'll take it that everything is fine then," Jim said. "Please ask for me if you need anything."

"Thanks, Jim," Monica said.

Jim said hello to Monica, whispered something in her ear, and then walked off. The three men didn't go away though. Monica pulled Percy aside.

"What's going on?"

"I'm just trying to figure something out."

"You should be at home resting. I'm in the middle of work right now, but would you like me to take you home?"

"I like your hair."

Her cell phone rang.

"I'll call you tonight," Monica said. "Get some rest. Go home."

She scurried out of the lobby while talking on the phone. Percy went back to the three men.

"You weren't supposed to be there," the walking-cane-man said.

"We want to let you in on a secret," Barlow said.

Percy told them to follow him to the hotel restaurant. They sat in a corner booth. The three men ordered coffee, and Percy ordered a glass of iced tea.

"There are a lot of things you don't know about your Macy," Barlow said. "She's a lot dirtier than you think. You think we're bad. She was just as bad."

Percy gulped down the iced tea.

"She has things. Things that don't belong to her. And we were there to get them back. She is, at least, a thief."

Percy's right leg shook up and down.

"What kind of things?"

The three men took sips of their coffees at the same time, which made Percy think about synchronized swimming. Stay focused, he told himself.

"It goes back to Zephyr and our service in World War II. Remember how, one night, we were talking about how each of us had brought back something valuable from overseas."

Percy realized who the two other men were: Walter and Carl. It all made sense to him. Macy said that Carl had moved to South Carolina, and the license plate of the Buick was from South Carolina. The man with the walking cane must be Walter.

"You're Walter and Carl," Percy said.

They nodded.

"Hi," Walter said.

"Hello," Carl said.

"Macy was killed by her best friends."

"Nothing is as it seems," Barlow said. "We didn't kill her. Perhaps we should discuss this some other time, when you're cool-headed."

"Nothing is at it seems," Percy said. "So what is it exactly? Why didn't you just ask for your items back if she stole them from you?"

"Again, let's meet at another time. How about Thursday? That gives you two days to cool down, today and tomorrow. We'll meet here at ten in the morning."

Percy agreed. They stuck out their hands, but he didn't shake them. He placed a couple of dollar bills on the table for the iced tea and walked away.

27

Back at Macy's house, Percy started to look for clues, but he didn't know what kind of clues he was looking for. He wondered what would happen to Macy's house and her belongings. He went into Macy's bedroom.

The bed covers were strewn about, and all of the dresser drawers had been completely removed from the dresser. Clothes were on the floor—muumuus, shirts, dresses, shorts. There were figurines, framed pictures, and antique lamps on the floor—some were cracked and shattered, while others remained unbroken. There was jewelry everywhere. There were dresses and shoes. She had a fur coat. He laughed as he pictured her in this heavy, thick, brown fur coat. The size of it would seem to almost engulf Macy if she were to wear it. Percy parted the dresses to see if anything was behind them, but he didn't see anything. He went back to the living room and picked up the things that were on the floor. He threw away things that didn't have a chance of being fixed. He put aside two broken lamps to see if they could be fixed.

There was a knock on the door—Percy opened it and there was a middle-aged man dressed in a brown suit. He had black hair and wore dark black sunglasses. He was clean-shaven, and he held a tan briefcase.

"I'm William Fuller. I'm from the law firm of Farrell, Fuller, and Cosby. You must be Percy."

"I hurt my head," Percy said.

"It appears that we have some business to take care of—I'm sorry to hear about Macy."

They walked into the living room.

"I represent Macy. She has left you a good bit in her will," he said. "This includes the house and all of her belongings."

Percy scratched his head.

"She cared for you," he said. "When we completed these documents, she made it clear that she really loved you. Like you were family."

Percy became overwhelmed with sadness. He wanted to cry but held himself together.

"Family," he said.

They sat in the living room going over all kinds of papers. He had to give multiple signatures and initials—twenty-four in total. It took about an hour and a half. William told him that he would call if anything was left out, but everything should be okay.

"Thanks for your help," Percy said.

"Take care of her place—she trusted you."

William stood up and started to walk away before suddenly stopping.

"Oh. Wait. She left a letter for you, too. Or more like a note."

He opened his briefcase and pulled out a manila envelope. Percy took it from him—they shook hands and William walked out the door. Percy went back to the living room and sat on the sofa. He slowly ripped the edges of the envelope and pulled out a piece of paper.

Penelope,

Thank you for fixing my light bulbs. Thank you for helping me. Your company was greatly appreciated. I never told this to you, but you are much loved.

I'm assuming you're reading this after I am no longer around. Take care of yourself. You'll be fine. You should go to the pharmacy and see if you can find some decent allergy medicine.

Also, if you ever do find out, please know that it was because I was just bored, especially after Zephyr passed away. It wasn't for the money. I give it all away to charities, if that helps. I'm sorry if I disappointed you. In all honesty, I'm glad it's all over.

Find someone, and share your life with that person. Drink iced tea on the porch.

Again, thank you so much for being around. It was a great joy.

—Macy

Percy took a deep breath. His lips quivered, and he sat there on the couch rubbing his forehead. He was full of mixed emotions and wondered what this all meant. He needed some company—he couldn't gather his thoughts as he had just found out that he owned everything that belonged to Macy, and that she had done something that could disappoint him.

He went back to the hotel. He didn't know why though—maybe to see Monica, or maybe to confront Barlow and his friends again. Once he arrived, he remembered—Room Number 202.

He walked up two flights of stairs, breathing hard, and walked down the hallway a few steps until he came to room 202. Putting his ear against the door, he couldn't hear any noises. He knocked on it, but there was no response. He jiggled the doorknob, but it didn't turn. A hotel cleaning lady walked by. She wore black pants, a white collared shirt, white gloves, and a gray apron that had several pockets.

"Excuse me," Percy said. "I locked myself out of my room, would you happen to have a master key of something. I would go down to the lobby, but since you're here, it could make things a lot easier."

The lady looked at him and then took a ring of keys out of her pocket, and unlocked the door.

"If you will excuse me," Percy said. "I really have to use the bathroom."

He waited until she walked down the hallway with her cart full of cleaning items, towels, and bed sheets before walking in.

Barlow had two suitcases next to his bed, and there were a couple of carry bags on a cushioned chair. Above the bed was a framed painting of a sailboat in the middle of an ocean. On the writing desk, there was a small bottle of after-shave, a bottle of baby powder, a small stack of papers, and a golden watch. Percy took the gold watch and let it sparkle in the pocket of his jeans. He opened one of his carry bags and pulled out a trash bag—it had some of the items that belonged to Macy. The same could be found in the other carry bag. Why did they take these specific items? The two suitcases didn't have anything but pants, underwear, undershirts, and collared shirts. He took the two trash bags and left his room, throwing the gold watch into a trashcan as he walked back to his car.

28

Dear Zephyr,

I haven't heard from you in a while, and I am so worried. I have nightmares every night. But during the day—during the day, I dream about growing up as children together in our neighborhood. How innocent we were, especially in contrast to where we are now. I think about lemonade and bruises from playing on the street. Remember hide and seek? I could always find you, not because you didn't find a good hiding spot, but because you couldn't' stop laughing as you hid. All I had to do was listen.

I miss those days.

Please write back to let me know you're doing okay

.

As Ever,
M

Percy put the letter down on the coffee table and leaned back against the couch, lifting his head up toward the ceiling.

He imagined Macy and Zephyr playing on the street as children, or playing in the front yard of one of their houses, searching for four-leaf clovers. He saw them in the war, each at their separate stations, writing letters to each other. He envisioned Zephyr writing to Macy, using his helmet to cover the paper from the rain, with a flashlight propped underneath it.

Percy imagined Macy, late at night, in bed with her knees propping up a clipboard with an attached piece of paper as she was writing a letter to Zephyr. Everyone else was sleeping, but she stayed awake with a pen in hand and candle by her bedside.

He found a piece of paper and wrote his own letter to Zephyr.

Dear Zephyr,

My name is Percy. We have never met—we don't know each other, but I've heard a lot about you through Macy. She is now no longer here, and I miss her so much. You are no longer here either, and I wish that both of you could have spent more time together while being alive. It sounds like you two were quite a couple, and I can tell that Macy loved you with great intensity. And through your words and letters, I can tell that you loved her with just as much force.

I wish that I could've known you in person. I've never had a dad, and although I never physically met you, I feel like you could've been that figure for me.

I am now picturing you and Macy dancing in the clouds. There is jazz music playing in the background, and both of you are smiling.

Sincerely,
P. Winks.

Percy folded the letter and walked outside to the yard. He used Macy's lighter to set the paper on fire, waiting for it to burn until the flame reached his fingertips. He dropped the remains and stomped on it until the smoke subsided.

"Thank you," Percy said.

He walked back inside of Macy's house and stood in the middle of the kitchen, staring at the ceiling lights.

Percy was in bed in his apartment, looking at the afghan that Macy had given him months ago. He noticed something stitched into the afghan. He blinked and looked again, but before he could try to make sense of what it was, he closed his eyes to get some sleep.

Around two in the morning, he heard a shuffling noise outside of his apartment. He stood up and peered out the window—they were trying to be as silent as possible, in contrast to the loud, crashing noise they had made a few nights earlier.

Percy dodged the spots on the floor that made creaking noises and waited for them, hiding behind the bed. There were three of them. The door opened, and they went straight to the shelf using the light coming from outside. Percy popped out from behind the bed and pushed one of the guys, causing a domino effect, and all three men fell down. All three moaned and grunted. He picked up Walter's walking cane and began to lightly jab them in the stomachs and thighs.

"We want our things back," Barlow said.

"They're not your things," Percy said.

The three men stood up again. Walter propped himself against the sofa. He nicked all them on the shins with the cane. They winced.

"We're too old for this," Barlow said.

"But not too old to kill?" Percy said.

"We didn't kill her. She was already dead."

"She was already dead, so you stole her things?"

Barlow sat on the sofa and rubbed his shins. Percy turned on the lights in the living room and looked at him—he could see dark bags underneath his eyes.

"What is it that you're looking for?" Percy asked.

"Antiques. In particular, a model ship that Macy had in her house, but we couldn't find it."

Percy had taken it over to his apartment for safekeeping.

"We're old men now. We have nothing in our lives except bits and pieces of memories. We weren't as lucky as Macy, Zephyr, Janet, and Ted. We've lived poorer lives than them."

Percy remembered that Ted and Janet were the parents of the CEO whose vase was stolen.

"They've lived extravagant lives since the War, and we've had nothing," Barlow said. "They had the riches, while Walter, Carl, and I had to live on very little money. And now we want our turn."

"It's not their fault that your lives suck," Percy said.

"It is their fault," Barlow said. "That model ship I'm looking for doesn't belong to her. It's mine. That stolen vase claimed by the Wrights is mine. They all belonged to me. We can make a fortune off of it."

"Why would they steal it then?" Percy asked.

"They were jealous that I had received these gifts from the families we helped in Poland. Neither of them had gotten anything, and they knew that when they returned to Atlanta, they were going to try to win Janet and Macy over. They took everything from me. You see those two clowns?"

Barlow pointed to the two figurines Percy had placed on the shelf.

"Those aren't hers, they're mine. I gave a man in Poland some money to help him, and in return, he gave me those."

"Macy told me that Zephyr's grandfather had made that model-ship himself," Percy said.

"Because she didn't want to admit they had stolen it from me," Barlow said. "They did it so casually too—when we came back, and we were all at Janet's house opening up the things we had brought back. Carl and Walter had a few things to give to their friends and family, and I, of course, had some antiques, which included the model ship and the vase."

Percy thought about the letter Macy had written to him, and how she said she was sorry if she had disappointed him if he finds out. Perhaps this was what she meant.

Barlow stood up and walked around the room. He walked two full circles before sitting down on the bed.

"And whenever I unwrapped these things," Barlow said. "I could see the envy in their faces. Especially Macy and Janet. The next day, I had everyone over for dinner, and after that, I haven't seen any of these things up until now."

"Why didn't you take it back from them?" Percy asked.

"Because I never saw them actually take the things. I didn't want to accuse my best friends of stealing from me. I didn't have proof. It was a hunch, but a good hunch. And I was right. I figured if I came back and didn't see any of these things in Macy's house, I wouldn't say anything or do anything. But once I saw my things, I couldn't let her get away with it."

Percy noticed that Barlow was confident as he told his story.

"They didn't even ask," Barlow said. "I would have at least thought about giving some of the things to them, but instead, they snuck around my back and took them. And ever since the day my things went missing, Ted, Janet, Macy, and Zephyr ignored me."

"Was it you all who stole the vase from the Wrights?" Percy asked.

Barlow said that they were planning on it, but somebody had gotten to it before them.

"I wouldn't doubt it if Macy ended up stealing the thing," he said.

"But why are you so keen on getting these things years later?"

"Pent-up aggravation, and anger, son," Walter said.

The other two men nodded their heads.

"Don't call me son," Percy said.

"It wasn't even any of our things, but we were all close to each other," Walter said. "Barlow, Carl,

Zephyr, and the whole gang. It wasn't right, what they did to Barlow. And now seeing Barlow stressed out with financial problems, we felt that he deserved to get these things back."

"And what would you plan to do once you got these things back, Barlow?"

"The Antique Road Show," he said.

Percy loved the Antique Road Show—he was amazed by how much some of those things were worth without the owners even knowing it. It was his second favorite show after Oprah. He looked at Macy's antiques and realized that they could have probably gotten a lot of money for them.

"That's a good show," Percy said.

"They will be coming to Charleston soon," Barlow said. "And I figured if I could get these things back, I could make some money and live comfortably for at least a little bit. I deserve at least a little bit of happiness. The three of us would split the earnings, even though Walter and Carl refused to take any of the money."

"We are truly sorry about Macy's death," Carl said. "But after all these years of our pent-up grievances, it doesn't affect us as much as it affects you. Barlow, especially."

"How long will you all be in town?" Percy asked.

"We were thinking as long as it takes to get the things we want. But now, I think we're just getting sick of it all. Who knows?"

Percy almost felt sorry for them.

"I should turn you all in," he said.

He wondered again how much money they would get from selling the antiques. He guessed that they could probably live the rest of their lives off of many of Macy's possessions. He looked at the three men. He stared into each of their eyes. They were tired and hurting. They looked like weathered dogs waiting for their lives to end.

"You can go to the house and take what else you want."

They didn't say anything—they stood up and made their way to the door.

"Macy's house should be unlocked, take what you want. But don't throw things around and make a mess. Just take what you want, nicely, which you could have done the other night as well. You realize that none of this had to happen. There were several other ways of getting these things."

"Jealousy got the best of us," Barlow said.

"Just hurry," he said. "And I don't ever want to see you all again. If I do, I promise I will go to the police."

"What about the model ship?" Barlow asked. "That was the real reason for this whole thing."

Percy pulled the model ship out from underneath the bed. Barlow's eyes widened.

"This?" Percy asked.

"Yes, that's it," Barlow said.

Percy remembered when he had first seen Barlow and how laid back and sleazy he appeared. He would never have imagined him losing his cool, but his impression of him was erased as Barlow stood in front of him and stared at the thing Percy held in his hand. The other two men had stopped putting things in the trash-bag from Percy's shelf and were also looking at the ship. Percy handed it to Barlow. He cuddled it and took a few steps back. He held the ship up to the light.

"Bills will be paid now," Barlow said.

"Whatever," Percy said. "Just hurry up and go. You have a half-hour before I call the police."

They scurried to get the remaining things into the trash bags from Macy's house. Percy went with them. Barlow didn't help though. He held the model ship tightly in his arms while Walter and Carl filled their trash bags. Walter tripped over his walking cane that Percy had left on the floor in the living room. He stumbled into Barlow who almost dropped the model.

"Be careful," Barlow said. "We have to be careful."

An hour or so later, he watched their car leave the driveway. He tried to go to sleep after the men left, but he was restless in bed thinking about Macy. He didn't know Zephyr, so he didn't really care about whether he stole something or not, but he thought about Macy. Would she really steal so many things from her friends? As long as he knew her, she seemed to be an honest lady. Maybe she had grown to be a decent person, and her past, in the form of Barlow, Walter, and Carl, had come back to haunt her. He got up and looked at the remaining things belonging to Macy.

He started looking through drawers for bills, letters, or any other types of mail. She didn't have too many. He saw a couple of envelopes addressed to or from M.M.C. He had never heard Macy mention anything called M.M.C. Percy put those aside to look at later. He found an address book in one of the kitchen drawers. She didn't have too many phone numbers in the organizer. The Wright's phone number was listed. Taped to the inside of the back cover was a sheet of paper with M.M.C. written on it. Under it was a long list of phone numbers and addresses. He wondered why she hadn't put these into the regular part of the address book.

30

When Percy heard a knock on the door of his own room above Macy's garage, he didn't know what to do. It was the first time someone had knocked on his door. The few times Macy would go over to his place, she never knocked—she would just walk in. He looked around his room. He hid underneath the bed when he heard another knock. He closed his eyes and thought about ice cream before hearing a voice coming from outside. It was a gentle voice, calling his name. He crawled out and stood up, brushing off his pants, and whispered.

"Hello," he said.

There was another knock.

Percy walked toward the door and knocked back.

"Are you there," he asked.

"Yes," the voice said. "I am here."

He realized that he was the one who was supposed to open the door. Slowly turning the knob, he peered over from the side of the door and saw a lady wearing blue jeans and a blue shirt. She had shoulder-length black hair and black eyes. Percy thought that she was pretty, and he couldn't manage to speak.

"I'm Penelope," she said.

"Damn," Percy said. "I thought I was Penelope."

"I thought you were Percy," she said.

"Why yes," he replied. "Yes, I am Percy."

He opened the door all the way and waved at her.

"I don't know you," Percy said.

"You don't," Penelope replied. "But we have a mutual connection."

"Ice cream?"

"What's that," Penelope said.

"Do we both like ice cream?"

"I think so," she said. "I love mint chocolate chip."

Percy raised his eyebrows—he kept his excitement to a minimum.

"This must be our mutual connection," he said.

"It could be. But we also have another connection."

Percy looked confused and then started to nod his head.

"Yes," he said. "And waffles."

"Not exactly. Well, yes, I guess so. I like waffles, too."

"So nice," Percy said. "With syrup."

"And blueberries," she said. "But that's not what I mean. Macy."

"I'm sorry," Percy said. "But she is no longer alive."

"I heard the sad news."

Percy looked at her, not knowing what else to say.

"I'm her niece."

Percy didn't know that Macy had any siblings—she had never mentioned any kind of family member to him apart from her husband.

It took a few seconds for the surprise to settle in.

"I didn't know she had anyone else."

"I'm Penelope."

"I really thought I was Penelope."

Penelope tilted her head, confused. She went on to tell him that she was the daughter of Macy's sister.

"They were very close at one time," she said. "But they had a huge falling out—to the point that they stopped talking to each other. I miss her. She was a sweet aunt when she was around."

"I understand," Percy said. "She was like a mother to me."

He realized that they were still having their conversation at the door—she was still standing outside.

"Should I go out?" he asked. "Or do you want to come in?

"Whichever is best for you."

"Let's go sit on the porch of Macy's house."

There, Penelope explained to Percy about her mother and Macy's relationship.

"They were inseparable for the longest time," she said. "But then they stopped talking to each other. I don't quite understand why."

Percy looked at the porch fan twirling amidst the summer heat and thought about his time spent with Macy outside of her house. He missed her, and Penelope had become his closest connection to her. He asked her what he thought happened between the two.

"All I know is that my mom, Margaret, didn't agree with something that Macy was doing."

This statement made Percy raise his eyebrows. He looked around as if he was about to tell a secret, making sure that no one else was around.

"Have you heard of M.M.C.?" he asked.

She shook her head and pulled out a cigarette, reminding him of Macy.

"Do you mind if I smoke?" Penelope asked.

"Please do."

"I haven't heard of M.M.C.," she said.

"I haven't either, but I'll find out."

"Maybe we can find out," Penelope replied. "Together."

Percy went on to talk about what he had noticed or found out over the past few days and mentioned the three strange men who recently appeared—Walter, Carl, and Barlow, and how the initials, M.M.C. could be seen on various belongings of Macy.

After Penelope left, Percy stayed on the porch, trying to let his encounter with Macy's niece settle in. Why didn't Macy tell me about her sister and Penelope, he wondered. As time continued to pass after Macy's death, she became more and more of a mystery to him. He didn't know what she had been up to, what secret life she had lived, but he knew it was something connected to M.M.C.

He liked Penelope and looked forward to seeing her again. When he offered Macy's house to her as inheritance, she declined, saying that she liked living in Chicago and that he deserved the house more than anyone else. She was an architect, and once she found out about Macy's death, she took a vacation to come to Atlanta to see if there were any unresolved matters.

"My mother is no longer alive," she had said. "So I'm the next of kin, I guess."

She told Percy she found out about him through Macy's lawyer and was glad to hear that not only did her aunt have a good friend, but also that there was someone to take over her residence and belongings.

Percy pretended that Macy was sitting across from him, having an imaginary conversation about her niece.

"She's nice," he said. "Reminds me of you."

He sat there and talked for a half-hour, not noticing the neighbors walking by, staring at him in confusion.

"Why didn't you tell me?" he asked.

Once he finished his conversation, he went back to his place, thinking about waffles and ice cream.

To Percy's pleasure, Penelope visited him again soon after their first encounter. This time, they went inside Macy's house. He pointed to the ceiling lights in the kitchen.

"It was a struggle," he said. "But I was able to replace the light bulb."

He then went on to show Penelope the various letters and belongings connected to M.M.C.

"What do you think?" he asked.

"It must be some kind of organization," she said. "And look at all these items listed. They seem like antiques—pieces of history."

Percy told Penelope about the three men and how they would frequently visit Macy, and that on the night she died, they were looking for a particular item.

"Maybe they were just trying to steal antiques and sell them," she said. "There's a lot of money to be made in the antique market."

"From what I understand, they didn't kill Macy, but she had already died of personal health reasons. They all seemed like friends. Why steal?"

"It's too late in the day," she said. "But let's visit some of these local antique stores and see if they know anything."

Penelope had been staying at a friend's house in Atlanta, but Percy noticed that she looked tired, and it was well into the night.

"If you wish," he said. "You can stay here or at my place."

"That's very sweet of you," she said.

"Sweet," Percy said.

"But I'll be okay—it won't take me long to get back to my friend's place. I promised I'd watch a movie with him tonight."

"Him?" Percy asked.

"He's a friend from college."

"I have a friend from college, too," he replied.

"You're cute," Penelope said.

"Cute."

She hugged him and said that she would see him again soon. Percy didn't go back to his place—he took a pillow from one of the couches and lay down on the kitchen floor. He felt guilty. He really liked Penelope, but at the same time, he felt like he was betraying his feelings for Monica.

Penelope, although it happened in a short span of time, was the only person since Monica whom he really liked on a personal level. He had to reveal his guilt and called Monica around 2 a.m. She picked up the phone and answered in a quiet voice, a voice full of sleep. Percy was excited that she had picked up, not realizing the time, and almost shouted back to her.

"It's me. Percy. How is everything? What are you doing? Are you okay?"

"What time is it," Monica replied. Are you okay? Are you hurt?"

He looked at the clock, which read 2:07.

"Oh wow," he said. "Sorry—I didn't realize the time. Were you sleeping?"

"Yeah—I need to get up early in the morning for a meeting, but it's fine. Is something bothering you?"

Percy was about to say yes, but hesitated.

"I just wanted to speak with you."

"What about?"

"I might almost have a nice friend," Percy said.

"That's great. That's really great."

"But I feel guilty," he said.

He paused. Monica asked why.

"I feel like I'm betraying you."

She again asked why.

"Because apart from you and Macy, I've never really had any close friends. I've never wanted to be friends with anyone else. And the fact that she's a lady—I feel guilty."

Monica reassured Percy that it was perfectly fine to have more friends and that he should have more friends.

"I'm happy for you," she said. "But who is this mysterious lady?"

Percy explained to her about his encounters with Penelope and that she was Macy's niece.

"Do you think you all will go out on a date?" Monica asked. "Sounds like you really like her."

"Date? I don't think I've ever been on a date before."

"This is a perfect opportunity. Ask her out."

"How? Should I get down on one knee?"

"Just stand on both your feet, or you can be sitting down, too, and ask her if she wants to get dinner and watch a movie."

"Thanks for talking to me," Percy said. "It really means a lot. And I'm glad you're happy for me."

"I am," she said.

There was silence before she spoke again.

"I really am."

After they had ended their conversation, Percy felt much better knowing that Monica liked that he might possibly have a new friend. However, he almost wished that she wasn't happy. He went back to Macy's kitchen and lay down on the floor, the couch pillow under his head. He looked at the ceiling light bulb and sneezed.

32

Percy met Penelope at the city park. Penelope had suggested earlier that they meet there for lunch. Percy wondered if this counted as a date. He was both nervous and excited. He bought a sandwich tray and made some ramen and put it in a large thermos. When Percy arrived, he saw that Penelope was already there, with a huge spread upon a blanket. He walked up with a big smile.

"I made you a thermos," he said. "It's ramen, with hot sauce. I also have a tray of sandwiches."

He liked that Penelope looked pleased.

"Great," she said. "I brought some food, too."

Percy looked at the spread and saw a variety of foods. He saw pasta, French bread and cheese, ribs, chicken wings, salad, and a jug of water and a jug of iced tea.

"You've brought so much," he said.

"Enjoy. Come, sit."

Percy sat down next to her and they started eating. Percy went for the wings first.

"The ramen is full of flavor," Penelope said.

"I made it myself," Percy said. "I think the flavor is brought out more because it's in a thermos."

Percy enjoyed Penelope's response to the food he brought as he moved on to the pasta.

"What was Macy like?" he asked.

"I couldn't have asked for a better aunt," she said. "When she was around, she was very sweet, kind, and giving. I felt like I had a personal bond with her despite the chaotic relationship she had with my mother."

"She was nice," Percy said. "She was my mentor and friend."

"You all must have gotten pretty close. I'm glad you all were able to enjoy each other's companionship. I honestly didn't know if she had any friends here."

Percy nodded his head as he chewed on a rib.

"I've been thinking," Penelope said. "About M.M.C. and all that you've shown me, and I really think we should visit some of the local antique stores to make any kind of connection."

"Antiques," Percy said.

"There's one not too far from here. Let's check it out after we finish eating."

They ate quietly, but Percy didn't feel awkward or nervous. It was a good quiet as he listened to the sounds of the park while finishing his ribs. He liked how Penelope ate—slowly, as if each bite was carefully thought out.

"The ramen was delicious," she said.

"It's basically fresh from the stove. I put hot sauce in it, too. Have you heard of boudin?"

Penelope said she hadn't, and Percy explained it to her and was pleased with her fascination for the food.

"I wish you could try some."

Once they were finished, they picked up and headed toward the antique store. Percy read the shop sign.

"Southern Antiques and Collectibles."

They walked inside and were greeted by a man wearing a yellow collared shirt and khakis. His brown hair was thinning, and he had a strong jawline.

"Let me know if you need any help," he said. "My name is Evan."

Penelope looked around the store.

"Do you know someone named Macy Thorpewaite?" she asked.

Evan looked at the floor, thinking. Percy looked at the floor, too, pretending to think. Evan shook his head.

"I'm afraid I don't," he said.

"Have you heard of any kind of organization with the initials, M.M.C.?" she asked.

Evan looked at the ceiling. Percy did the same.

"M.M.C.," he said. "I can't say that I have."

"Thanks—we'll just walk around a bit."

"Thanks," Percy said. "It was nice talking to you."

Even nodded his head and smiled before walking away.

Penelope gently grabbed Percy by the wrist and led him around the store. Percy breathed hard as her physical touch was one of the few times someone had actually made contact with him. He thought about the times Monica had hugged him and tapped him on the shoulder.

They stopped at a section full of teacups and various tea accessories. The thick, dusty air made Percy sneeze repeatedly.

"Dust."

Penelope laughed and told him to be careful not break anything while he sneezed. Percy picked up a teacup and turned it upside down. His eyes widened.

"Look."

Penelope saw the M.M.C. initials in fine print on the bottom of the teacup.

"Is it a brand?" she wondered.

She took the cup and walked to Evan who was behind the counter. She showed him the initials.

"Odd," Evan said. He sighed. "I have never noticed that. Is it named after your friend, Macy?"

She was about to reply, but Evan interrupted her.

"I'm sorry," he said. "But we are about to close for about an hour for lunch, but you're welcome to come back then."

He held out his arm to guide her to the door. Percy looked at Penelope and noticed her buried eyebrows—she looked angry.

"Percy," she said. "We're getting kicked out."

"What did I do?" Percy asked. "I have allergies."

"Please," Evan said. "Come back later. It's time for a lunch break. Please understand."

They walked out and heard the door being locked. Percy looked at the store hours posted on the door.

"It doesn't mention a closing time for lunch in their hours. How would people know?"

"Exactly," Penelope replied. "We'll be back."

33

Percy realized that Penelope was true to her words when she knocked on his door at 2 a.m. This time, he didn't hide under the bed. He had a good feeling that the person was Penelope. When he opened the door, he saw Penelope dressed in all black, including her hat. She held a bag.

"Why are you up?" Penelope asked.

"I'm awake."

"But were you sleeping? Or were you already awake when I knocked?"

"Come in," he said.

Penelope sat on the bed as Percy noticed her tight black spandex pants.

"Ever since I've left the shelter," he said, "I've lost my sense of security and don't really sleep more than three or four hours at a time."

"Shelter?"

Percy explained to her his upbringing, and how he didn't know his parents and that he grew up in a shelter until he was eighteen.

"No one really wanted to adopt me."

He noticed Penelope's watery eyes and felt bad for making her tear up.

"But it's good," he explained. "Because I don't think I would've ever met Macy if I had a different life."

He paused.

"Or you."

Penelope stood up and walked toward Percy, putting her hands on each side of his face.

"Has anyone ever kissed you?" she asked.

Percy looked down at the floor and then up at the ceiling.

"Kissed?" he replied. "How come?"

"Because I want to kiss you," Penelope said.

Percy had a quick vision of Macy's garden.

"What are your thoughts on marigolds?" he asked.

"I love them."

"That's what I imagine what a kiss would be like."

Penelope leaned in and as she was about to kiss him on the lips, there was a loud knock on the door, startling Percy, causing him to bump heads with Penelope. She grunted with the short flash of pain. Percy tripped over himself and fell. Penelope couldn't help but to laugh. She helped him up.

"Was that a knock on the door?" he asked.

Penelope nodded her head.

"But you're here," he said.

He looked around the room and then closed his hands.

"Get ready to fight," he said.

There was another knock. Percy opened the door quickly, with one hand cocked back, ready to throw a punch. Before him stood Allen.

"I was getting worried," Allen said. "You haven't been answering your phone."

Percy looked at his phone, seeing the red light blink repeatedly.

"Phone," he said.

He motioned for Allen to enter—Penelope put up her hand to say hi.

"Oh," Allen said. "Is this a new friend, Percy? She's cute."

He nudged Percy with his elbow. Percy nudged back. Penelope introduced herself.

"I'm sorry to hear about your aunt," Allen said. "I heard she was a great lady. Percy really looked up to her."

"I'm sorry about your aunt, too," Percy said.

Percy apologized for missing his calls. He also explained to him about M.M.C. and their quest to figure out what it means. He told him about the visit to the antique store.

"Curious," Allen said.

"Curious," Percy said.

Allen looked at Penelope and then at Percy and then back at Penelope.

"I'm glad you're well," he said. "Let me know if you need anything. I should get back to bed. Sorry for the bother."

Percy thanked him as Allen said bye to them.

"He's been a really good friend," he said. "I don't have too many of those."

"You now have another good friend," Penelope said.

He realized the late time, looking at the clock next to his bed.

"I love that you're here," he said. "But how come?"

"You have any black clothes? I was thinking we'd go back to that antique store."

"I think it's closed right now."

"Exactly," Penelope said.

Percy realized what she meant, especially with the black clothes, and became hesitant.

"For Macy," Penelope said.

"For Macy," Percy said.

He went to his dresser and pulled out a black t-shirt.

"I don't have any black pants."

"I thought the same," Penelope replied.

She opened her bag and pulled out a pair of black pants.

"They're for women," she said. "But they will still fit you. They're baggy. Try it on."

Before Percy could go to the bathroom to change, Penelope walked up to him.

"Let me help," she said.

Percy just stood in front of her, not knowing what she meant.

She took off his shirt and helped him put on the black shirt. He felt embarrassed. It was the first time he had been bare in front of anyone—especially in front of someone of the opposite sex.

"Here," she said. "Try these pants."

Percy looked at the bathroom, wondering if he should go in there to change, or if it would be okay to change in front of her.

"I won't look," she said. "If that makes you feel more comfortable."

Percy just needed to hear her reassurance.

"It's fine," he said.

"It's not like it's the first time I've seen someone undress."

"It's my first time to undress in front of someone," he said.

"You're sweet," Penelope said.

Percy unzipped his jeans and took them off as Penelope handed him the black pants. He thought about Monica but didn't feel guilty this time. He felt excited as if he was riding a bike for the first time on his own.

"I haven't ridden a bike in years," Percy said.

Penelope looked surprised, not knowing where Percy's comment came from, but she went along with it.

"Me either," she said. "Look. They fit just fine. I think they look nice on you."

She picked up her bag.

"Let's go before it gets too late," she said.

"Or too early, I guess," Percy said.

They took Percy's car, but Penelope insisted on driving.

"I love to drive, too," Percy said. "Road trips and all."

"You should come to Chicago, and maybe we could take a road trip together."

Percy was about to suggest a visit to New Orleans but refrained from doing so. That was a trip he would only make with Monica and Bill, or by himself. When they reached the antique store, Percy felt ill. He knew he was doing something wrong, illegal, and the only way to convince himself to continue was by thinking about Macy.

"Hold on," he said.

He walked over to the edge of the curb and started dry-heaving. Penelope rubbed his back.

"It'll be okay," she said. "I promise. You're here with me."

Once he stopped coughing, the quietness of his surroundings became more apparent as there wasn't a sound to be heard. Even the insects are sleeping, he thought.

"To the side door," Penelope said. "I noticed that the side door was just locked by a hook when we were there earlier today."

"Do you do this often?" Percy said.

"Only a few times," she said. "But it's always for a good cause. Plus it keeps life exciting—sometimes the day job can be a bit of a drag."

"Me, too," Percy said.

"Really?"

"No, not really. This is my first time."

"You've had a few firsts today," Penelope replied.

"I almost once tried to break into a place not too long ago," Percy said. "At a newsstand."

"What happened?"

"I ended up losing my watch."

She smiled—Percy could see her teeth shining white in the darkness and the reflection of a distant streetlight in her eyes. As they walked to the side door, Penelope pulled out a thin strip of metal.

"This should slide right through," she said. "And as I move it up, it'll unhook the latch. Almost forgot, we should put these on."

She pulled out two pairs of black gloves.

"Don't want to leave a trace."

Penelope quietly slid the metal slip through and moved it up—it caught the hook and made a clicking sound as it tapped against the door after being unlatched. Percy was impressed by how well Penelope's plan was going.

"Here's the deal," she said. "If an alarm goes off, we run straight to the car and take off without looking back. Got it?"

"I have it," Percy replied. "What about cameras?"

Penelope said she looked for them when they were there earlier but didn't see any. She opened the door as Percy took a deep breath and closed his eyes, hoping that an alarm wouldn't go off. He exhaled.

"Nothing," he said.

"Good," Penelope said. "We're good."

They walked in—Penelope pulled out two flashlights and gave one to Percy.

"But now what do we do?" Percy asked.

"We are going to take note of as many items as possible that have M.M.C. and compare them to the list at Macy's house."

"I could go for some waffles," Percy said.

"Sounds good," Penelope replied. "We'll get some breakfast after."

They spent about an hour and a half there—they couldn't get every item but had a good sample of antiques with some kind of M.M.C. inscription. Percy had started to sneeze incessantly as the dust and overall antiquity of the place took its toll on him.

"Sneezing," Percy said.

"Poor thing," Penelope replied.

After they left the antique store, much to Percy's pleasure, they found a 24-hour diner and ate chicken and waffles. They couldn't stay for too long as Penelope had to go back to her friend's place so her friend could use the car for work. He worked in the shipping and loading department of a large furniture store, and he usually had to go in early, before the store actually opened, to make sure the inventory was on schedule. As they switched cars at Percy's place, Penelope gave him a hug.

"That was a nice night," she said.

"It was fun. The chicken and waffles were great."

She gave him the notepad with the list of items from the antique store.

"I'll be over soon, but if you'd like, you can get a head start."

Percy watched as she drove away. He knew he should go to bed but was too wired, yet he was too tired to compare lists at Macy's house. He thought about calling Monica but refrained from doing so. He went inside his place and sat down on the foot of his bed and watched the sun fully make its appearance before finally falling asleep.

34

The day after their visit to the antique store, Percy decided to compare the list that he and Penelope made at the store to the list at Macy's house. He called Penelope to let her know, and she said she'd meet him there but to not wait for her.

Percy was able to make some connections, much to his excitement. On Macy's list, there would be an item, then a selling price, and then the initials S.A.C., which Percy figured meant Southern Antiques and Collectibles as the price on Macy's list matched the price they had written down for the same items they recorded at the store. Though the connection was there, he still didn't know what it meant.

Percy updated Penelope when she arrived in the early evening, and she was equally as excited.

"It has meaning," she said. "But what is the meaning—that's the problem."

Just as Percy was about to respond, Monica entered the house. As soon as he saw her, Percy stood up so quickly, he almost looked like he was doing a jumping jack. He was happy to see her and shouted her name. Monica said that she was driving through and just wanted to drop by to check in on him. He looked at Penelope and then at Monica and introduced them to each other.

"Percy told me about you," Monica said. "Nice to finally meet you."

"Nice," Percy said.

Penelope looked at Percy and smiled.

"You didn't tell me that you had a girlfriend, Percy."

She turned to Monica.

"Nice to meet you, too."

Percy blushed. He was embarrassed by Penelope's statement, but Monica explained that they were longtime friends.

"He's certainly blushing though," Penelope said.

"He's just shy," Monica replied.

Percy managed to speak and told Monica what they were doing, but he didn't mention that they broke into an antique store, thinking she'd get mad. He showed her the connections he had made, but when he looked at Penelope, he noticed that she looked annoyed for not being shown the list instead. After all, it was Penelope's project, he thought. He motioned to Penelope.

"Come see."

"I'll take a look at it later," she said. "Show it to your friend."

This gave Percy a sinking feeling, realizing that Penelope wasn't liking the situation. He didn't know what to do—he didn't want to hurt Penelope's feelings, yet at the same time, he was happy to see Monica. By proximity, he bumped Monica's elbow as he showed her the list, and he could smell the freshness of her hair and skin. She must have just showered, he thought. He wanted to tell her that he liked the scent of her soap and shampoo, but he didn't want to cause any more annoyance with Penelope. All this time, he somewhat wanted Monica to be frustrated that he had another friend of the opposite sex, but he now realized that he was worried that Penelope's feelings would be hurt in relation to his friendship with Monica.

"The connection is there," Monica said. "But what does it mean?"

"Exactly," Percy said.

Penelope sighed.

"I did some research," she said. "Between police reports and newspaper clippings."

She turned to Percy.

"That's what I wanted to tell you. These items on both Macy's list and our list have at one time been listed as stolen, either as residential or commercial property. But the items were eventually retrieved, as stated by the original owners, and so the police stopped their search."

"Feels like some kind of ring operation," Monica said.

Percy didn't quite understand what was going on but spoke as well.

"Exactly," he said.

"How are your injuries?" Monica asked.

Percy was happy to see that Monica cared about his well-being. He nodded his head.

"I'm dandy."

"Dandy?" Penelope replied.

She laughed.

"I don't think I've ever heard someone actually use that word."

"No need to tease," Monica said. "It's a nice word. I like it. It explains how he feels."

"I wasn't teasing," Penelope said. "It was just a comment."

There was silence and Percy could sense tension.

"Let's check some other antique stores," he said. "Southern Antique and Collectibles can't be the only shop connected to these initials."

Both Monica and Penelope nodded their heads in agreement. Penelope was the first to leave, saying that she'd call him later. She didn't say bye to Monica as she left, which made Percy feel bad. He turned to Monica.

"You don't like her," he said.

"She didn't really give me a chance to like her. I don't think she likes me, especially when she thought we were together."

"Just friends," Percy said.

"But I'm glad that you all are friends. It looks like she really cares for you."

"Is that okay with you?" Percy asked.

"It's great," she said. "Just be careful. Sometimes things don't go the right way. I just don't want your heart to be broken."

"Don't worry," Percy said. "I think I've been through quite a bit since I was a child. I am not invincible, but I find ways to manage."

"I know you do," Monica said.

She smiled and put her hand on his shoulder, making Percy breathe hard.

"You are invincible in my eyes. Let me know how it goes with this whole antique extravaganza, and if I can help. I'm glad you're okay."

She hugged him and left. Percy remained standing in the middle of the living room, holding the lists. He looked at the lamp next to the couch and stared at it until his legs became tired.

"M.M.C.," he said. "Macy's Magic Committee. Macy's Meaningful Connection. Magic Macy Corporation."

He left the house and went back to his place.

<h1 style="text-align:center">35</h1>

Percy thought about his last encounter with Walter, Carl, and Barlow at the hotel. He wanted to have another talk with them, but this time, with Penelope so as to not feel like he was being ganged up on. One Penelope equals all three of them, he thought, plus, she's smarter than me and more aggressive.

They went to the hotel lobby counter and asked the lady if she could call Walter—he remembered his room number from the time he had snuck into his room.

"Please tell him that Percy is waiting for him in the hotel restaurant."

Percy looked to see if he could find Monica, but she was nowhere to be found.

"Monica works here," he said.

"You really like her," Penelope said.

"She's my closest friend and the friend I've known the longest. She was the first person to really care for me."

Penelope was drinking a gin and tonic. Percy wanted chocolate milk but the restaurant didn't have any—he was drinking a glass of milk with strawberries to get as close to a strawberry milk as he could. He poured in a few packets of sugar to sweeten it up.

"Did you all ever date?" Penelope asked.

Percy shook his head.

"How come you all never dated?"

"We're just really close friends. And I don't know how to go about seeing if she wanted to. She's with someone now."

Percy looked out through the entrance of the restaurant, into the lobby, watching people walk back and forth—some were with families, others were just by themselves. He looked at those either checking in or checking out as they stood next to their suitcases.

"I can watch people all day," he said. "Do you not like Monica?"

"I just didn't get a chance to like her or not like her. I don't think she liked me though."

"She was just surprised," Percy said. "I think, aside from Macy, I've only had two other friends, Monica being one of them."

Percy drank his glass of milk and strawberries.

"I really like you," he said.

He was surprised that he said that aloud and was embarrassed. That was meant to be a thought, he thought.

"I really like you too," Penelope said. "You're nice. Most guys I've dated or been around have been jerks for the most part."

"I can be a jerk," Percy said.

"Sure you can."

"What about the friend you're staying with?" Percy asked.

"Tyler?" Penelope replied. "Oh, he's just a longtime friend—like how Monica is to you."

"Have you all ever dated?"

He took a big gulp of his milk and strawberries and wiped the top of his lip.

"We did. A long time ago, but we decided that we are just better off as friends. He's a nice guy—you all would be good friends."

She started to light a cigarette but saw a No Smoking sign. Percy pointed to an area across the restaurant.

"Look. There's a smoking section."

"It's fine," she said. "I should quit or cut down or do something like that."

"Are you single now?" Percy asked.

"Yes sir. I like being alone for right now, but every now and then I'll have some fun."

She smiled and took a sip from her gin and tonic.

"Grin and tonic," she said.

"Same here," Percy said. "I'm not dating anyone either."

He had never been on a date, but he didn't want to let Penelope know that. Penelope tapped his wrist.

"Good for you," she said.

They sat there quietly, looking around each other. Percy wanted to make eye contact with her when he could tell that she was looking at him, but he felt too shy to do so. Their awkward silence was saved by Walter, Carl, and Barlow walking into the restaurant. Percy thought that he would never be happy to see those three men, but he felt less shy once they arrived. The three men pulled up chairs to their table, making a loud noise.

"What a horrible looking group of men," Penelope said. "Who are you?"

They each said their names.

"Who are you?" Barlow asked.

"I'm here as Percy's friend, and I want to ask you some questions."

"Why should we answer to you?" Walter replied.

"I have a strong connection to the police, and I know that you all have stolen items," she said.

She turned her head to where they couldn't see her face and winked at Percy. She gave him a slight tap on his leg with her foot. Percy couldn't tell if she was lying or not.

"That's why you should answer to me," she said. "But if you don't want to, we can go, and I'll give my friend a call at the station."

She stood up.

"Come on Percy."

Percy stood up, too, both excited and confused.

"Wait," Walter said. "What do you want to know?"

Percy and Penelope sat back down.

"Why did you all gang up on my friend here?"

Carl coughed before he spoke.

"He got in the way."

"No he didn't," she said.

"No I didn't," Percy said.

"All he did was protect Macy's belongings, all of which now belong to him," Penelope said.

"We took what belonged to us," Walter said.

"That's precisely my point," Penelope said. "Idiot. All of Macy's items belong to Percy now. Either way, it's breaking and entering, and theft, until proven otherwise."

"Not if she had already stolen these things from us," Carl replied. "It didn't belong to her in the first place."

Walter stood up. Percy became nervous, wondering if there was going to be another fight. He clenched his fists just in case. Penelope noticed it, and lightly tapped Percy on the leg to let him know that it would be okay.

"It looks like our presence here is of no use," Walter said. "Especially if we're here for you to harass us. We've done no wrong."

"Sit," Penelope said. "Don't be a coward. I have another question for you all."

Walter looked at Barlow and Carl, who remained sitting. They motioned to Walter to sit back down.

"What?" Walter asked.

"You're pretty," Percy said.

"Thanks," Barlow said.

"Not you," Percy replied. "That was meant for Penelope."

She put her hand on Percy's shoulder.

"Thanks. I haven't heard that in a while. It means a lot."

"This is very sweet and touching and all," Walter said. "But we're leaving."

"Sit," Penelope said.

He sat down and the waiter came to the table asking if they would like any more drinks. The three men asked for a shot of vodka. Penelope asked for another gin and tonic, and Percy said he was fine. He was too caught up in the moment to enjoy another sweet beverage. Plus, his stomach was starting to hurt.

"What do you want?" Walter asked. "We're about to leave this place and go back home. We're done here. Leave us alone."

"What do the initials M.M.C. stand for?"

Walter looked at Carl and Barlow.

"That is none of our business," he said. "We know nothing about that."

"Looks like you do. Is it an organization? A club? What does it have to do with Macy?"

"You'd have to ask Macy," Walter said. "And it looks like that would be a bit tough to do so . . ."

"Honestly," Carl said. "We don't know. I've vaguely heard of it during this past visit but . . ."

Percy saw Walter give Carl a tap on his foot and Carl stopped talking.

"Our hands are legally tied," Walter said. "We can say no more."

He leaned in close and whispered.

"But you might want to check this antique store called The Teacup."

He stood up and the other two men did the same.

"That's it," he said. "We've got to go. Percy. It may not look like it, but I am sorry for your loss. Macy. She was quite a lady."

"I understand," Percy said.

"It was a pleasure meeting you all," Walter said.

The three men walked away as Penelope took another sip. Percy noticed her glassy eyes.

"The Teacup," he said.

"Sounds like another visit to an antique store."

She finished her drink, taking one big gulp.

"Feeling it a bit," she said.

Percy told her that she could take a nap at his place. Penelope agreed, and they drove back to his garage apartment. She immediately went to sleep in his bed. Percy didn't know what else to do— whenever he was in his room, he was always in his bed as he didn't have any other furniture. He stood in the middle of the room, wondering if he'd ever see Walter, Carl, and Barlow again. He wondered if they were being genuine or deceiving. He wondered what did they really know about M.M.C. He looked at Penelope and realized that she had taken her top off and was sleeping in her bra.

"Wow," he said. "That's a real live bra."

It was the first one he had seen in person, on someone.

"Amazing," he said.

Not knowing what else to do, he left his place. He wasn't worried about leaving Penelope behind because she had kept her car in Macy's driveway, so she could drive back to her friend's place once she awoke.

36

Percy was feeling overwhelmed. He had too much going on in his mind. The death of Macy, Monica being back in town, his divided feelings between Penelope and Monica, the three men, Allen—he couldn't remember the last time so much had taken place in his life. He was used to slowness and inactivity, and all of a sudden he found himself in one big blur.

He decided to exercise for the first time in years, spontaneously, while walking across the park to the coffee shop. He was wearing pants and casual shoes but decided to exercise anyway. He pulled one knee up to his chest in an effort to stretch but kept losing his balance. He bent down, keeping his legs straight, and tried to touch the grass but couldn't get past his shins.

The summer heat was at its peak, and Percy had worked up a sweat before even starting his impromptu workout. He breathed hard as he looked around and did five jumping jacks and four push-ups. By now, Percy was covered in sweat—he went for a jog, and after about three minutes, he had to stop, gasping for air. He bent over, watching the sweat drip from his face to the grass. He stood up straight and put his hands behind his head and looked around, still panting hard. He managed to speak to himself in between hard breaths, giving advice to himself.

"Rest," he said. "Sit and rest."

He tried to control his body, but he couldn't stop, and toppled over onto the ground where he lay on his back. He stared at the sky before him, seeing birds fly over him amidst the clouds. He felt like he could've fallen asleep there despite his body being drenched in sweat. His breathing finally calmed, and he sat up, wiping his forehead with his shirt. He stood up and felt fine, but as he started to sneeze, he also started to dry-heave.

In between his bouts, he would look around. He saw a few people looking at him. He waved.

"Hi," he said.

A lady asked him if he was okay.

"I am. I just needed to clear my head."

He coughed a few more times before his bouts subsided. Percy sighed and continuously wiped the sweat from his face. He saw another person look at him and Percy waved.

"Time for some coffee," he shouted.

As he walked into the café, everyone was staring at him. Some of the customers moved aside to let him get ahead in line as he looked like he was in dire need of water.

He ordered an iced mocha and a bottled water and took a seat at a table next to a stand containing various local newspapers. He picked up the *Atlanta Chronicle* and read an article updating the stolen vase:

Vase Is Still Missing

Leads on the stolen vase are slowly on the decline much to Ted and Jennifer Wright's dismay. A statement from the police reads as follows: "The more time passes, the more of a chance that the vase is long gone. However, we're being patient. At some point, there's got to be some kind of sale or a mistake, and we'll be sure to be on it. The Wright Family have been model citizens here in Atlanta and have made valuable contributions to the community in a variety of ways. We hope to find them the justice that they deserve." The stolen vase, a family heirloom, survived WWII and eventually made it here. The family has offered a reward in regards to the vase. Please contact the *Atlanta Chronicle* or the police if you have any information pertaining to the stolen vase.

Percy thought about the vase and wondered if it had anything to do with M.M.C. Did Macy steal it? The three men claimed that Macy had stolen some of their items. But if so, how? He wished Macy was still alive for a myriad of reasons, including to defend herself against such accusations.

"Explain," Percy said. "Please let me know."

37

They were sitting in the outside area of a pizza restaurant. Percy thought it was too hot to sit outside to eat a food like pizza, but he knew how much Monica loved being outside, especially when eating. She told him how she was always stuck indoors and that she would feel suffocated at times. Percy didn't mind it all too much because he could watch the cars driving by as well as people walking by.

He hadn't seen or heard from Penelope since the day she took a nap at his place after having too much to drink—it had been a few days, but Percy figured that she was busy spending time with her friend. He was surprised, after only knowing her for a short span of time, by how he already missed her, and he became sad as he thought about how eventually she would go back to Chicago.

"What's wrong?" Monica asked. "You seem down."

Percy wiped the sweat off his forehead and rubbed his thighs with the palms of his hands.

"I wish I knew where every one of these cars is going, and these people walking, I wonder where they're going. So many people. So many places. So many backgrounds, and I will never know."

Monica sipped her water.

"I have something quite important to tell you."

The waiter came outside to take their orders. They decided to split a large pizza—half and half. Percy got a vegetarian, and Monica got the meat lovers deluxe. The waiter walked away.

"Is it about the weather," Percy asked. "Is a storm coming?"

Monica shook her head. Percy sipped his iced tea and thought how Macy's iced tea was the best.

"I wish you could've met her," he said.

"Who?"

"Macy. You would've liked her, and she would've liked you."

"I wish so, too."

She was about to speak again but became hesitant.

"How's it going with Penelope?" she asked.

Percy's mood immediately shifted for the better—his eyes lit up.

"Wow," Monica said. "I take that as it has been going well."

"She's neat," Percy replied.

"Have you asked her out on a date yet?"

"Should I?"

"I think so, Monica said.

"How so?" Percy asked. "Should I go down on one knee and ask her?"

"You're not proposing to her!" Monica exclaimed.

She started to laugh, but then she quieted down and looked into the sky.

"You know," she said.

Percy noticed that she looked humbled or embarrassed.

"That's a great idea," she said. "And it's your idea. And if that's how you want to ask her, I think it would be lovely."

Percy appreciated her comment, and he was amazed at how over and over again, Monica was always there for him, supporting him, looking after him.

"You're swell," Percy said. "I hope before she leaves for Chicago, we all can spend some time together. Maybe we could go for a movie or get dinner or break into a store."

"Break into a store?"

"Just a thought," Percy said.

He noticed that her voice changed tones—not the solid, confident voice that she usually exhibited, but much more lighthearted, almost sympathetic.

"Did you want to talk about the weather?"

"Not quite," Monica said. "Macy was like your mother, right?"

"I think so."

"You think so because you never had a mother."

Percy flinched.

"I'm so sorry," Monica said. "That came out the wrong way. I didn't mean it like that."

Percy didn't look at her and stared into the street.

"Percy," Monica said.

He continued to not look at her.

"Percy."

He looked down at the cement ground, noticing a caterpillar slowly making its way over a leg of the table.

"Percy."

He sighed and looked at Monica.

"I'm sorry," he said.

"For what," Monica said.

Her voice quivered.

"What are you sorry for?"

"I'm sorry for never having a mother."

Monica's eyes became watery.

"I really didn't mean it like that," she said. "There is no reason for you to be sorry. I really didn't mean it that way. Please let me explain what I meant."

"Excuse me," Percy said.

He stood up and started pacing back and forth in front of their table, staring at the sky. His mouth was moving, as if he was talking, but nothing could be heard.

"Please sit," Monica said. "As your closest friend, please sit for me."

Percy stopped pacing and looked out into the street, caught in a daze with the flow of cars driving by. He sat down and tightly grabbed the cloth of his pants.

Monica tried to put her hand on his shoulder, but he moved back to where she couldn't reach him. He rocked back and forth. Monica apologized over and over again, and Percy finally came to a calm state.

"What I meant was that I can't imagine how life would be to grow up without a mother. You've been through so much, and so much I don't know."

Percy looked at her and sipped his iced tea.

"Before I go on," Monica said. "Please tell me about your childhood. I've always wanted to ask you, and I feel like we're such close friends now, that I would ask you."

"We are close friends," Percy said. "And I understand your curiosity."

The waiter came with their pizza. He set it in the middle of the table and asked if they needed anything else. Monica shook her head, and Percy waved to him. He breathed in the smell of the pizza and sliced a piece to put on his plate. He saw the green peppers, onions, mushrooms, and his mood started to lighten up. Monica took a slice of her side of the pizza—covered in pepperoni, sausage, ham, and bacon, and put parmesan on it. Percy bit into his and spat it back out onto the plate and gulped down his drink.

"Did you burn your tongue?" Monica asked.

"It burns," Percy said.

They both waited for a bit for the pizza to cool down—Percy was drenched in sweat and wished that the outside ceiling fans were more effective.

"Please tell me," Monica said.

Percy began to explain his upbringing, going into detail as to how he didn't realize that he didn't have a mother until he learned how babies were born. When he was at the shelter, a boy named Cookie explained to him about sex and reproduction.

"He was a bit older than me," Percy said. "And he knew a lot more about life than me. I was literally sheltered."

"Were you all friends?" Monica asked.

"More like he was a big brother to me," Percy said. "I was more familiar with the idea of brothers and sisters than children and parents. He wasn't my actual brother of course, but the concept of family was completely different at the shelter than at a home."

He looked at his slice of pizza, waiting for it to cool down.

"I remember asking Cookie if I had a mom, and he said yes, and he said he does, too, but that we don't know them because we grew up at the shelter."

"Do you still keep in touch with Cookie?"

Percy shook his head.

"I wish. He left before me and I took it badly, cried. He found parents, or rather parents found him. He told me that he would keep in touch and visit, but I asked him not to, because it would be too hard for me. He left and kept his word."

Percy went on to say that he asked one of his counselors about his parents, but she would never give him a concrete answer.

"We're your family now," Percy said. "That's all she would say."

"So you never knew your mother at all?"

"No memory at all. Cookie said that she most probably gave birth to me real young or I was unplanned, and she sent me to the shelter for a better life."

Percy went on to explain that after Cookie left that it wasn't the same at the shelter. He started to get picked on more often—both verbally and physically.

"Sometimes the counselors would catch and stop them," Percy said. "But then they just became sneakier with their bullying. I'm glad I went through it, though, because it made me tougher."

Percy wasn't much of a smoker, but he wished he could have one as he talked to Monica, as well as an alcoholic drink, but he wasn't much of a drinker either. One of his legs kept shaking as he was trying to deal with his nerves. It was the first time he had gone into detail about his upbringing. He sighed.

"It feels nice," he said. "To let this all out to you."

"I'm glad," Monica said.

"And it was then," Percy continued. "After Cookie left and with all the teasing and taunting I experienced, I learned how to be comfortable being alone."

Percy told Monica how he read a lot of books, most of them were books kept at the shelter.

"I did the whole read a book under the bed covers with a flashlight thing. It was fun—I felt like I was doing something adventurous though there wasn't really any danger at hand. Just someone telling you to go to sleep."

Percy wanted to eat a slice of pizza, but he couldn't get himself to do so as he lost his appetite. He noticed that Monica hadn't eaten yet either.

"And I was good with being alone," he said. "And then, you know."

"What do you mean?"

"Then I was able to get into college and meet you and Bill," he said. "It was nice."

Monica smiled. Percy looked at the tip of her nose and noticed how it was smooth and round, natural.

"It still is nice," Monica said.

Percy asked Monica if she was still in touch with Bill. He had lost touch with him soon after they all graduated.

Monica told him she would email or talk to Bill from time to time.

"He's doing well," she said. "He's married, living in Tallahassee. He's in real estate, and from what I can tell, he's quite successful."

"We should all get together and take a road trip one day," Percy said.

"I need you to be patient with me," Monica said. "With what I'm about to tell you. I mean well with what I'm about to say, and I don't want to you to get angry."

"I can never be mad at you," Percy said.

"While you have been doing your research in relation to Macy and those initials, I was doing a bit of research myself."

Percy's leg was still going up and down. He looked at Monica's hands—both were fiddling with a napkin, tearing it into small pieces. It was the first time Percy saw Monica appearing nervous.

"I've been thinking about you a lot lately," she said.

"Thinking," Percy said.

"I really hope you don't mind."

She sat back, letting go of the tattered pieces of the napkin. Percy started thinking about boudin. Before Monica could speak again, he talked.

"I really do have a plan. It may not seem like much right now, but I do have a plan to be self-sufficient and have a solid job."

Monica inquired what he was talking about and Percy explained how he intended to open a boudin café using the money Macy had left him. Monica was supportive.

"Maybe you can help with the marketing aspect," Percy said. "We can be a team."

"I would love to," she said. "This could be a nice business for you."

"And then I would like to open a few more and have some kind of local chain."

Percy told her that he knew that it would be risky and take a lot of work, but he was confident in the possibilities.

"There's nothing to lose," he said. "If it doesn't work, I can find something else—I don't need much to live. I've become quite a good gardener, too, and maybe I could open a nursery of some sort. I can also fix light bulbs."

"I admire you," Monica said. "And I think it will work. What would you call this place?"

Without hesitation, Percy told her.

"Macy's Boudin Café and Iced Tea."

Monica said she liked the name and encouraged him to go for it.

"I will definitely team up with you," she said.

She leaned in forward, grabbing the pieces of the napkin.

"Back to what I wanted to tell you."

"I promise," Percy said. "I won't get mad at you—I trust you. Tell me."

"My boyfriend was a big help with this, too.".

"Boyfriend?"

"Oh," Monica said. "I may have forgotten to tell you, but I have a boyfriend. He's great, and we will all have to meet soon, but more on that later."

Percy didn't like the idea of how a person he had never met, who even worse was Monica's boyfriend, would be a part of this important conversation Monica wanted to have with him. He just wanted it to be between the two of them.

"What about Penelope?" Percy asked.

"I'm sorry. But I didn't tell her—I wouldn't know how to either. And I didn't feel comfortable doing so because we still don't really know each other."

"Comfortable," Percy said.

He thought about how uncomfortable he felt in that Monica's boyfriend knew, and not Penelope. The pizza was cold, but Percy and Monica had yet to touch their meal. The waiter came in to check on them and looked confused.

"Are y'all not liking it?" he asked.

"It's great," Percy said.

"But you haven't had a bite yet."

"It looks great."

"Do you all want to try something else?" the waiter asked.

"We're fine," Monica said. "We're just in the middle of catching up, and we have a lot to talk about. It's not the pizza."

"It's us," Percy said.

The waiter said he'd be back in a bit to see if they needed anything else.

"It was great talking to you," Percy said.

The waiter walked away.

"Percy," Monica said.

Percy thought about how Macy used to call him Penelope.

"Through some contacts," Monica continued, "we were able to find your biological mother."

Monica looked at him and waited for a response, but Percy didn't speak. He just looked at her chin.

"Percy."

"Who?"

"Your mother."

"My mother?"

"Yes, Percy. We found her."

Percy became quiet again.

He wasn't mad or happy—he didn't know how he should be. Monica looked at him, more confused than Percy.

"Well?" she said.

"Wishing well."

"What do you think?" Monica asked.

"Do you like Picasso?"

Monica leaned back, appearing to be agitated. She took a deep breath. Percy noticed her distorted face. A couple sat down next to them. Percy focused on the man's shoes—they were green and white with blue laces.

"Blue," he said.

"Percy," Monica said. "Please. I need you to stay focused. Do you understand what I just told you?"

Percy shook his head.

"Your mother," she said. "The one that gave birth to you. We found her. She's here in Atlanta."

As Percy remained quiet, Monica went on to explain how she found her and why. Her boyfriend had a contact in social services, and she was able to go back to the time when Percy was left at the shelter and find the record for his mom. Normally, that kind of information isn't usually given out, but her boyfriend was close enough to his contact, and she gave it to him.

"And I have it now," Monica said.

"Did your boyfriend laugh at me?" Percy asked.

"Why would he laugh at you?"

"Because I grew up in a shelter and he didn't."

"He's not like that," Monica said. "Trust me. I wouldn't be with a guy like that. He's nice. Like you. But that's beside the point. What do you think?"

The waiter came back and checked on them, and Percy asked for the bill.

"Just one check," he said.

"Would you like a to-go box?" the waiter asked.

Percy said no and Monica said the same.

"Sorry," Percy said. "Didn't mean to waste the food. It looks great, but I lost my appetite."

"Me, too," Monica said.

"It happens," the waiter said. "No need to apologize. I'll be right back with the check."

Before the waiter could walk away, Percy changed his mind and asked for him to come back.

"How about a to-go box?" Percy asked.

He asked Monica if she was sure that she didn't want any of the pizza and she said she didn't want any. The waiter said he'd be back with the to-go box and the check.

"Do you think you'll meet up with her?" Monica asked.

"But why?" Percy replied. "Why would I want to get in touch with her?"

"I understand," Monica said. "That's a good question. I just thought maybe you could get some closure and at the same time, reconnect with your mother. Maybe it could be good."

"I feel like the closure already happened when she sent me to the shelter."

Monica understood and agreed with his comment. She was being patient and understanding of the delicate situation.

"I just thought it would be of interest to you—to understand why she let go of you."

The waiter came back with the check and the to-go box.

"Thank you," Percy said.

"Please come back and eat," the waiter said.

"It can happen," Percy replied.

The waiter walked away, and Monica reached for the bill, but Percy took it before she could get a hold of it. She contested but eventually gave in and thanked him.

"This is all my pleasure," Percy said.

He was trying to be cheerful. He signed the check and started to get up, baffling Monica.

"Wait. Where are you going?"

"I guess I'll go back to my place. Feeling tired."

Monica asked him to sit down just for a few more minutes.

"But really. What do you think about finding your mother?"

Percy sat back down and looked at the couple next to them—the lady was smoking a cigarette. Percy leaned in toward her.

"Hi, I'm Percy."

He waved.

"I'm sorry to be a bother, but I was wondering if I could have a cigarette?"

She said no problem and gave him one. Percy leaned back again, realizing that he didn't have a lighter. He leaned toward the lady, and she was ready with a lighter.

"Very kind," he said. "Sorry again."

He lit the cigarette.

"You smoke?" Monica asked.

Percy coughed, causing his eyes to water—they became red.

"I guess not," she said.

Percy sipped his watered-down drink and took another drag.

"Macy used to smoke," he said.

"Please focus," Monica said. "I know it's tough, but what do you want to do about your mother?"

"Why? Why would I want to meet her? My life has been great without her. There's no need to intrude in her life—there's a reason why she left me at the shelter. She didn't want me for whatever reason."

Monica nodded, showing that she understood his reasoning, but she continued to go deeper.

"What about closure? Or what about finding out what really happened. Maybe all this time, she wanted to talk to you, but she couldn't find you."

Percy inhaled a deep drag of his cigarette and coughed. His eyes were still red and watery. He looked drunk. He again asserted that he felt like there was closure when she left him at the shelter. Monica continued to debate.

"But what if that's not the case?"

Percy took another drag, shifting his head, looking at the sky. He didn't answer. Monica took out a piece of paper and pushed it toward Percy.

"Here's her information. Just in case. Please, take it. For me."

The "for me" part always got Percy.

He took the piece of paper, and without looking at it, not even to see his mother's name, he put it in his pocket.

"No rush," Monica said. "I'm not asking for you to do it right now, but when you feel like you're up for it. All in all, I think you'll be glad that at least you tried."

"What if she doesn't want to talk to me or meet me?"

"That still counts as closure, I think. You can totally just move on just like you've done. But if she wants to talk to you—that would be amazing."

"Thanks," Percy said. "I know you're doing this because you care for me. It must have been tough."

"I do care for you. And even though I thought that it would be tough, I felt comfortable because it's for you."

"For you."

They both stood up and hugged each other.

"Thanks for the pizza."

"Thanks."

They parted ways—Percy, with his to-go box in hand, went one way, and Monica went the completely opposite way. She turned around and shouted.

"I'll see you soon," she said.

Percy turned around.

"Hi Monica."

Before going back to his place, Percy drove to the area where his shelter was located. He remembered seeing quite a bit of homeless people there as a child and always felt sad for them, sometimes crying to his counselor, wondering why they didn't have a place to stay while he did. He hadn't been in that area for quite some time and became nostalgic as he saw some of the familiar buildings and streets. He thought about visiting the shelter but decided against it as he was already full of emotions. Everything looked the same.

He found a parking spot and got out with the pizza, and walked down a few blocks until he found someone cuddled up in a blanket, leaning against the wall of a convenient store that had been closed down. He was sleeping. Both the man's beard and hair were a combination of gray and black. Next to him were a few grocery bags which looked full. Percy wanted to wake him up and say hi, but he kept quiet. He put down the pizza box right next to him and walked away.

"Be well," he said.

38

When he got back to his apartment, Percy didn't bother taking off his clothes or shoes and went to bed. He wasn't so much physically tired, but he was emotionally drained. He was trying hard not to think about his mother, and his conversation with Monica, but he couldn't get it out of his head. What if she hates me, he wondered, or what if she doesn't even remember me? He went to sleep as soon as his head touched the pillow and dreamt about boudin.

MACY'S BOUDIN CAFÉ AND ICED TEA
Hours:
Monday - Thursday 5:30 AM - 10:00 PM
Friday - Saturday 5:30 AM - Midnight
Sunday - 7:00 AM - 5:00 PM
<u>Dishes</u>
Boudin Links
Boudin Balls
Boudin And Waffles
Macy's Boudin Special [Boudin Over Chargrilled Oysters]
Boudin Sandwich [French Bread, Boudin, American Cheese, Hot Sauce, Relish—Add Turkey or Chicken]
Boudin Enchiladas

Boudin Egg Rolls
Boudin Kolaches
Boudin Crab Cakes
<u>Sides</u>
Caesar Salad
Fries
Chips
Scrambled Eggs
Fried Pickles
Asparagus and Grits
Potato Salad
<u>Beverages</u>
Water
Iced Tea
Soda Pops

Percy slept through the night with ease for the first time after the longest time. When he opened his eyes the next morning, he realized that his arm was around another body. He immediately sat up, eyes wide open. It took him a moment to realize that he was at his apartment. He pulled down the covers a bit to see who he was sleeping next to—Penelope. He had been so tired and was in such a deep slumber, he couldn't remember if he met with Penelope the night before.

He tried to remember if he had woken up in the middle of the night to let Penelope in, or if they had a conversation at all. Nothing came to mind. He looked at Penelope and saw that she had taken off her top, sleeping in her bra just like she did last time.

He could smell her vanilla-scented hair and found it refreshing. As he got out of bed, he realized that his shirt and jeans had been taken off, and he was in his boxer-briefs. His shoes and socks were on the floor. Did I take them off, he wondered, what exactly did I do last night? What happened? Why are my clothes not on me? I wish I could have some boudin right now. He put on his jeans and shirt, not knowing if he should awaken Penelope. He did a push-up and stretched his legs.

"Penelope," he said.

She didn't stir.

"Penelope, hi. It's me, Percy."

She continued to sleep. Though he was surprised that she was there in his bed when he woke up, he was glad. He wanted to tell her about how he had his mother's contact information. Perhaps, she can give me some added advice, he thought. He also wanted to see if she had any updates about M.M.C. He called her name again. Nothing. He sneezed, and Penelope started to flutter he eyes, waking up. She stretched her arms and moaned. She saw Percy and sounded excited.

"Good morning," she exclaimed.

"Hey, it's me, Percy."

"Good morning, Percy."

She talked as if she had been awake for a few hours. She got out of bed and Percy saw that she had taken her pants off, too, as she stood in front of him in her underwear.

"Wowsers," Percy said.

"What?"

"You're very pretty."

He sneezed while trying to say "underwear." She was wearing a matching red set. He thought that Penelope would realize that she was barely clothed in front of him and start to put on her clothes, but she sat down on the edge of the bed, scratching her stomach. Percy tried not to stare, making repeated glances at her body.

"It's okay to look," Penelope said. "After all, I am here in front of you."

Percy changed the subject. Penelope yawned.

"How come you're here? What happened? I don't remember talking to you at all last night."

"You were pretty out of it, sweetie."

"Sweetie."

She told him how she wanted to drop by because it had been a while since they had met. As Percy assumed, she had been spending time with her friend.

"When I knocked on the door, and you didn't answer, I figured you were sleeping. I was too tired to drive back to my friends' place. Luckily, your door was unlocked."

"You probably could've broken in with ease anyway."

"True."

"Why are my clothes not on me? I missed you."

He looked at her stomach muscles and belly button. For the first time, Percy didn't feel guilty about betraying Monica.

"You were dead tired," Penelope said. "But I thought you'd sleep better if you had your shoes off. So I took them off. Then I thought you'd sleep better if your jeans were off. So I took them off, and then your shirt."

"And I didn't wake up."

"I was surprised, but not at all. You were out of it big time. At first I thought you were super drunk, but I didn't smell any alcohol from your breath."

"Super," Percy said.

He repeated the word "super" a few more times. He was still amazed that Penelope was there in front of him, casually sitting in her underwear, talking as if they were at a coffee shop or restaurant.

"I guess I had one of those sleeps coming," he said. "It had been a while."

"I must say," Penelope said. "You have a nice body. When I took your shirt off and saw those tightly packed chest muscles, I was very attracted."

"I did a push-up today."

"And I missed you, too."

Percy breathed in deep and sucked in his stomach.

"But don't get me wrong," Penelope said. "I'm not just about physical looks—I look to see if a person is good, kind—natural. And you are."

"I can be strong," Percy said.

He exhaled, letting his stomach go back to its original state.

"I have so much to tell you. I'm glad you're here."

Before Percy continued with what he wanted to say, both he and Penelope asked each other if there was any progress made about Macy or M.M.C. Both said no.

"But I will be persistent," Percy said. "I am determined."

"Be determined," Penelope said. "I am here to help you."

Percy, surprising himself, sat down next to Penelope, looking at her thighs. He wanted to put his head on her shoulder. She noticed him glancing at her legs, and made them more apparent to him. Percy tried to talk but couldn't as he was lost in her legs.

"Do you think I'm a good person?" Penelope asked.

Percy tried to look at her eyes, but couldn't. He looked at her chest and then at her neck then at her chin. He finally managed to look into Penelope's eyes.

"You have been very kind to me," Percy said. "And understanding and patient with me. I don't think you're a good person. I think you're a great person. Thanks for being my friend. Inside and out, you're beautiful."

"If only you really knew me," Penelope said.

She laughed.

"Thanks, Percy."

For the first time, Percy saw Penelope's softer side, almost vulnerable. She pressed her shoulder against Percy's, and Percy wanted to put his arm around her but refrained from doing so.

"How do you not have a girlfriend?"

Percy realized that he had a solid excuse.

"I guess I just have too much going on right now."

That led to Percy telling Penelope about his conversation with Monica and how he had his mother's contact information. She listened intently, with her mouth open—her eyes, watery. Percy tried his best to look at her chin.

"I have her number," he said. "What should I do?"

Penelope spoke in a soft voice.

"What do you want to do?"

"Most of me doesn't want to do anything, but a little of me wants to call her."

He watched Penelope as she ran her hand through her hair, making it look more kempt.

"You really are pretty," he said.

It was supposed to be a thought, but to Percy's surprise, the words came out.

"I've heard that from time to time," Penelope said. "But I think you're the only one who means it."

She adjusted her legs, crossing one over the other. Percy asked again what she thought he should do. Penelope said she felt uncomfortable giving him advice about this, because she could never imagine his situation, and what she, herself, would do.

"I understand that Monica means well," she said. "But that's tough."

Percy realized that Penelope didn't quite agree with Monica getting into his private affairs, but he defended her, reassuring Penelope that Monica was his closest friend and that she really cared for him.

He saw Penelope's facial expression, which tensed up, and he also reassured her that he cared for her, too, and that was why he was asking her for her input.

"You're my new friend. I hope one day you and Monica can really get to know each other. You all would make good friends, I think."

"I guess I come off as that I don't like her," she replied. "But that's not the case. I'm just trying to understand your friendship with her. I know you like her in a different way, in the sense that you wish you all were together."

Percy's voice was strong and confident.

"I think I'm getting over her."

"You probably think I'm jealous. I'm not. I'm just trying to figure it all out."

Percy, not realizing what he was doing, put his hand on her thigh. He felt the warmth of her skin and quickly removed his hand. Penelope took his hand and put it back on her leg. Percy envisioned Macy saying "posture" to him which made him straighten out his back as he kept his hand on her thigh. Penelope ran her hand through Percy's hair, causing him to be completely lost. He was flooded with random memories—the shelter, Monica, Macy, Penelope, the three men, movies, New Orleans— visions flashed in his head. He tilted his head down and stared at the floor, feeling the tips of her fingers against his skull.

"Do you really want to know what I think?" Penelope asked.

She took her hand, the one that was running through his hair, and put it on Percy's thigh. He nodded his head.

"I think you should get in touch with her."

"Why?"

"She's your mother."

"But she left me?"

"But you didn't leave her."

It was that last statement, though he didn't quite know what it meant, that won him over.

"I didn't leave her," he said.

"You didn't."

They talked a bit more, and Percy was fully convinced by Penelope that he shoul contact his mother.

He looked at her bra and then her underwear.

"I like that you're looking," she said.

She uncrossed her legs, and Percy felt dizzy. He sneezed.

"I'll think about it some more," he said. I just have way too much going on right now."

"Sounds like a great plan."

Percy said he was going to check out another antique store and asked her if she would join her.

"I won't be able to, today. But keep me updated. I feel like we're onto something."

She stood up and stretched her body. Percy did the same.

"I'm going to take a quick shower," she said. "And I'll be out of here. Thanks for letting me sleep here."

"Thanks," Percy said.

He watched her walk to the bathroom, unstrapping her bra. She didn't close the door, which made Percy look away. He heard the shower being turned on, and she started to sing. He was amazed about how open she was about her body—he had never known anyone like that. He did a few jumping jacks before leaving the apartment.

39

Dear Macy,

I miss you so much. I wish you were here right now as I have so much to tell you, and I need your advice.

You have been a great friend and mother to me. I don't have too many friends, and I never had a mother, so you meant a lot to me.

I don't quite know what you did, maybe I'll find out one day, but either way, no matter what, I will always defend your name. I'll let you know what happens though.

A few things: I plan to open a boudin café named after you. I've met your niece—why didn't you tell me? She's amazing. Things have been going well with Monica, too. Being with Penelope helped me to realize that it's time to release my feelings for Monica. She will forever be my closest friend.

I have my real mother's contact information. What should I do?

I'm patiently waiting for a light bulb to go out so I can fix it for you (it's still your house in my mind even though you gave it to me).

I hope you're well. I miss you.

—P

Percy folded the letter and threw it into a fountain full of coins. He went to an antique shop that was not too far from where he lived. It was a small family-owned store. The place made him sneeze.

"How are you doing today?" the lady who worked at the store asked.

Percy asked her if she knew Macy. She didn't recognize the name. Percy described his late friend's features to her, but she still didn't know who he was talking about.

"We don't have too many regulars," the lady said. "Sometimes, there would be a group of ladies who would come in and look around about once or twice a month. But they would never buy anything. They would just walk around and then they would leave. I would try to make conversation with them, but they didn't seem too cordial. I haven't seen them in the past couple of months though."

Percy looked around, pretending to be Penelope. He looked for any other entrances and if they had any security cameras just in case he and Penelope broke into this place as they did with the last store. He asked her about the cost of the two teacups he was looking at, and she said it was about two hundred dollars for the pair. He noticed in the back corner of the store a man was standing on a ladder, and he was installing something in the ceiling.

"Putting in security cameras?" Percy asked.

"We did an inventory recently, and there were a lot of items missing," the lady said. "There seems to be a few thieves that visit this store."

He told her that he would be back some time with some items to sell. She sounded excited about the idea of new antiques.

"It's been a while since anyone has brought anything new to this store. We've been losing money slowly these days. But we find ways to survive."

Percy met Monica at the sandwich shop near her work. She was sitting with another guy, who was dressed in a black business suit. He had short brown hair that was gelled and spiked. Percy didn't know that someone else was going to join them. He didn't want anyone else to join them. His name was Will— Monica invited him to dinner. He had shiny white teeth. Monica told Will about Percy's unfortunate experiences during the past couple days. Percy could tell that Will didn't really care but was trying to be polite.

"Sorry," Will said.

"Not your fault," Percy said.

Percy noticed his dark blue eyes and strong jawline. He was probably an athlete of some sort, which would be a plus for Monica, who also enjoyed sports. He had broad shoulders and large wrists. Percy could tell that Will didn't want him there just as much as he didn't want Will there. Will was only interested in Monica. Percy couldn't blame him though. He worked in the same office as Monica, and Percy could see that they had gotten close. He would zone out every now and then as they talked about work-related things. As Percy poked his sandwich with a fork, he realized why Monica wanted him there. She wanted his approval. She must really like the guy, Percy thought. He acted nice to Will for Monica's sake. He would ask him a few questions, and look at him as he answered them. He laughed when they laughed, and he gave his input every now and then to make it look like he was interested in their conversation. Percy couldn't do it for too long. He thought about Penelope.

"Nice meeting you, Will," Percy said.

"Same here," he said.

He didn't look at Percy when he said it.

"Are you leaving?" Monica asked.

Percy realized that Will was the one who retrieved his mother's contact information for him. He sighed.

"Oh," he said. "Thank you for finding my mother's information. I feel embarrassed."

Will sipped his drink and gently wiped his chin with the napkin. He found Will's response to be nice and genuine.

"Not at all," Will said. "I can't imagine what that would be like. I'm glad I can help. I know you and Monica are really close—it was my pleasure."

Maybe I'm wrong about him, Percy thought, maybe he really is a good guy.

"I guess I should go now," Percy said.

"Have you figured out what you're going to do?"

Percy didn't want to talk about it in front of Will, whether he knew what he was going to do or not.

"Not yet," he said.

"Let me know if you want to talk about it some more."

Monica hugged Percy and he left the restaurant. As he walked to his car, the initials M.M.C. came to his mind. It couldn't have meant Mickey Mouse Club. She never mentioned anything about Disney or being a Mickey Mouse fan. He drove around a bit until he came to a shopping center that had an antique shop. He had never noticed any antique stores in town until Macy's death—now, they seemed to be popping up everywhere.

There were a few people inside the store. He looked around at the figurines, plates, dolls, and lunchboxes. He picked up an old metal Superman lunch box. It was red, with Superman fighting a crook on the cover. He opened it up, and it still had the matching thermos. The price tag read $65. As he put the lunchbox back on the shelf, he noticed something scribbled on a small tag on the back of it: "M.M.C." As he walked around the store, he noticed that there were several other antiques with the initials, just like the store he and Penelope had visited. Many of the dolls and plates had it, as well as a variety of kettles and pitchers. This place didn't have any security cameras, Percy noticed, and it had another entrance on the side of the building. He walked up to one of the employees. He was an older-looking man, who had gray hair only on the perimeter of his head, except for the front part. He wore thin-framed glasses, a blue-collared shirt, and khaki pants. Percy showed him the initials on the lunchbox. He tilted his head up a bit to look through his bifocals.

"Let's see here," he said. "I'm not sure. I've never seen these initials before."

"Is there any way you could find out?" Percy asked.

He called for a lady named Reggie. She walked in from the back wearing a black dress, black shoes, and black-framed glasses. She had brown hair that came to her shoulders, a small nose, and small lips. Behind her, in the office in the back, Percy saw a shadow against the wall, and then he heard a door open and close. The man handed Percy the lunch box and walked away.

Percy showed the lunchbox to Reggie and asked her if she had seen the initials before, or if she knew what they meant. She looked at the initials and then she looked at Percy for a few seconds without saying anything.

"Why do you want to know about this?"

"A friend of mine, who had just passed away, had some things initialized with M.M.C."

"Who's your friend?"

"Mrs. Macy Thorpewaite."

She didn't blink.

"Who's she?"

"She was my neighbor, as well as a good friend of mine," Percy said. "I used to work for her."

"I don't know anything about this. But I'll sell it to you for twenty-five percent off the original price."

"Are you sure?" Percy asked. "You seem to have quite a few things with these initials on it. It's odd that you wouldn't have noticed this before."

He pointed at a shelf with a display of plates and kettles.

"Are you a detective, or an officer or something?" she asked.

"I was just a friend of hers, and I was just curious about these three letters."

He kept pressing the matter. He was positive that Reggie knew something about the initials.

"Is it some kind of distributor of antiques or something?"

"So you were friends with Macy?"

"You know her? We became very close these past few months. And she died a few days ago. And her house was broken into. She was my neighbor. They were looking for antiques."

"I read it in the newspaper," Reggie said.

"Did you know her?"

Reggie looked around. Percy did the same.

"No."

The phone started to ring. Reggie walked to the counter and picked up the phone. As soon she hung up, she hurried off into the back, where only employees were allowed. Percy waited for about a half-hour, but she never showed up again. The older man who worked there asked Percy to leave because the store was about to close. Percy told him that he would come back for the lunch box.

As he went back home, he thought about Reggie. She is the key, or she knows something. Why didn't she come back after the phone call? Who called her? Maybe he and Penelope would have to give the place a visit during the middle of the night. His thoughts shifted over to Will and Monica. He was doing fine with letting go of his feelings for her, but seeing her boyfriend stirred his emotions again. He started talking to himself.

"I really am happy for you. He's a nice guy and I hope he treats you right."

He thought about the time when Monica was going through a rough relationship with her boyfriend and their bad breakup. He had gone over to Monica's to find her crying. It was the first time he saw her in tears.

"Never again," Monica said. "I need to change the way I view people. Never again. Nice guys from here on out."

Percy hoped that Will was one of the nice guys.

"Hey it's Monica. I was just thanking you for meeting us for dinner. I really wanted you to meet Will. I think he's a really nice guy. What do you think about him? Anyway, give me a call back whenever you have some time. Hope you're doing okay."

Percy picked up the phone to call Monica back, but after dialing the first three digits, he hung up. He went to Macy's house—he went to her bedroom and saw a small jewelry box filled with papers and envelopes. He skimmed through the papers and found a few letters. They were addressed to M.M.C. That was it. There wasn't any street address, zip code, or return address. On the letter itself, the greeting read "Dear M.M.C. Attendee." It was a thank you letter written by Macy. She was thanking someone for attending an event and for purchasing a crystal horse. The letter went on to say, "With your contribution, the M.M.C. will be able to continue in its efforts to showcase the world's hidden treasures in an extravagant manner, while supporting various organizations, making the M.M.C. a hidden treasure in itself."

On another piece of paper, Percy found a list of names, an item next to each name, and then an amount of dollars next to each item. He scrolled down the list and saw a Reggie Feray. He wondered if that was the same Reggie he had met in the antique shop. He looked at some of the items listed. It included a porcelain bowl, a mantle clock, two dolls, a chair, a cabinet, and a collection of china. The prices for these things ranged from $6,000 to $15,000. At the top of the paper was a date, which read June 8, 2007—that was a year ago.

He found another list, which consisted of names, antiques, and prices for the antiques. It looked liked Macy was doing some kind of inventory. He found one paper which was dated a few months ago. He didn't even know that Macy knew all these people. He wondered if she had a secret life. She would sleep late into the day for most of the week. But there were many nights when he and she would stay awake late into the night talking on the porch, which could very well explain her waking up late in the day. He wondered if she went to sleep after he left the porch. She could have lived her secret life during the night and early mornings. And perhaps as he would start working in the morning on her yard, house, or whatever task she asked him to do, she would be just going to bed.

As he walked back to the apartment, he saw a man and a woman walking away from his place—they looked like they were in their thirties.

"Can you help me with anything?" Percy asked.

"Are you Percy?" the man asked.

"Hi, I'm Percy."

He waved his hand. The man had short brown hair and protruding cheekbones. The woman had long blond hair and skinny wrists. She looked like she should be playing tennis. They looked familiar. Percy knew he had seen them somewhere before, but he couldn't recall where and when. He looked at the man's designer shoes, and the woman's red flip-flops. Her toenails were perfectly painted with a red polish. Percy pictured their faces in black and white.

"Are you the Wrights?" Percy asked.

They walked inside the apartment. Leo said that he had been calling him on the phone, but Percy never knew because he didn't leave any messages on the answering machine.

"I like to talk to the person, rather than the machine," Leo said. "It sometimes causes problems at work, but we all manage."

Percy asked them why they were looking for him.

"You knew Macy Thorpewaite, right?" Leo said.

"She would talk about you all," Percy said. "Mainly about your parents."

"We read about you in the newspaper and about Macy's death," Leo said. "My parents would always talk about her and Zephyr. They really liked them. And so we're just basically here to pay you our condolences. I guess we're just trying to bring closure to the lives of my parents. Macy was the remains of their childhood."

"You've been reading about me and Macy in the newspaper, and I've been reading about you and the vase. How's the search going?"

"We've been wondering if you could help us out in regards to the vase. We were wondering if Macy had ever mentioned the vase. If she knew about its location after it was stolen."

Percy told them she had mentioned it when she read about the vase in the newspaper, and how Ted had gotten it during World War Two.

"But as far as knowing any leads as to who could have taken the vase—she never mentioned anything."

"Did she ever talk about someone named Barlow?" Leo said.

Percy told them how Macy would talk about her childhood days and she would talk about all of her friends, including Barlow, Walter, and Carl.

He didn't tell them that they were the ones who had broken into Macy's house or that they were in town.

"He had called us," Jennifer said. "And he asked us about the vase. This was only a few days before the vase was stolen. His name seemed vaguely familiar when he spoke to me on the phone, and then I realized who it was after remembering all these conversations that my in-laws had about their old friends. But I would never think that they would steal it though."

During Jennifer's conversation with Barlow, he claimed that the vase belonged to him and that they should give it back to him. She told him she didn't know what he was talking about, and that she had to go.

"That was the last I had heard from him," Jennifer said.

"We were wondering if you could help us find Barlow because I am almost positive that he stole it," Leo said. "But we also have another suspect."

According to the Wrights, the Thorpewaites and Ted and Janet had a falling out.

"Both Macy and Zephyr had become fanatics of antiques," Leo said. "And they thought that the vase would be the perfect addition to their collection. They asked my father if they could buy it from him, but he refused. He wanted to keep it in the family. You know, one of those things that get passed down from generation to generation. The Thorpewaites didn't like that. They really wanted the vase, and they offered to pay a large amount of money for it. My father still refused to sell it to them. And after that, they were on bad terms."

Percy wondered why Macy never told him about this. He always heard Macy talk about them in a positive way. In the middle of the conversation, Percy thought about Monica. Why would she like a guy like Will and not him? Leo continued to talk.

"A few months after my father passed away, and Macy's husband passed away, she called us again asking for the vase. And again, I refused to give it to her. She was never happy about the whole situation."

"Are you suggesting that Macy somehow stole the vase from your house?" Percy asked.

He remembered his last encounter with Barlow and how he had also mentioned that Macy had probably stolen the vase. But he didn't think he could ever picture that happening. What was Macy up to all this time?

"It could be possible," Leo said. "And I don't mean to be disrespectful. It's just a thought. We're at a loss right now and considering all possible scenarios."

"And how can I help?" Percy asked.

"Have you seen anything in her house? Or could you look around to see if you could find anything about the whereabouts of the vase?"

He told them that he had gone through several of Macy's things and that he never found anything related to the vase.

"But I'll make sure to look again, if it would make you all feel better," Percy said. "She had a lot of antiques, and when the men broke into her house, some were taken and some were broken. But I'll make sure to check again—the thought never occurred to me that she had the vase."

They were happy with his suggestion. He felt bad for them. But, if Barlow's story was true, it never really belonged to them in the first place. Ted Wright, the father, took it illegally without Barlow's permission.

They gave Percy their phone number and thanked him for taking the time to talk to them. As they walked out the door, Percy imagined Macy sneaking around their mansion in search of the vase. She wore all black, holding a black bag, and wearing black sunglasses. He visualized her crawling around with night-sensitive binoculars. He remembered that one day, while he was working in Macy's garage, he saw her wearing all black. But that was after the vase was stolen, so there couldn't have been a connection— unless she had just pulled another burglary. He looked at the phone number the Wrights had written down for him. Leo had also written a small message along with the number which read, "please help us find it if you can." Percy wanted to help them, but there wasn't really much he could do. He was almost positive that Barlow didn't steal the vase, and the vase wasn't in Macy's house. He thought about other people who could have known about the vase. The person who stole it was only interested in stealing the vase, which meant that the person knew that the Wrights had the vase and where they kept it. The newspaper mentioned that nothing else was taken.

41

M.M.C.
#19 of 2007

Sanjay Robindra-----Porcelain Bowl---6,000

Mary Lyles-----Mantle Clock---7,000

Kerkin Ploughs-----Lady Doll---6,000

Dianna Denver-----African Doll---10,000

Linda Crefts-----Russian Chair---7,000

Reggie Feray-----Wooden Cabinet---11,000

Scott Nimes-----China Collection (from China)---12,000

Xiu Lao-----Lamp (Without Shade)---15,000

Alicia Cots-----Flower Pot---6,000

Mya J.-----Tea Kettle---6,000

Bill Hannigan-----Wooden Desk---5,000

Susan Laps-----Lamp (Blue Shade)---10,000

Kenneth Wren-----Bookshelf---4,000

42

Monica called—she wanted Percy to go over to her apartment for another dinner with her and Will.

"I may drop by for a bit," Percy said. "I have some errands to run."

"What do you have to do today so badly that you can't come by for dinner?" Monica asked.

Percy could tell that Monica was a bit agitated.

"I have to do some things regarding Macy."

There was a brief silence. Her tone softened a bit.

"Is everything okay?"

"I just need to do some paperwork, that's all. I'll give you a call later on tonight."

"It might be time to let go of this whole Macy thing," she said. "It seems like it's taking its toll on you."

Percy didn't respond.

"Is it because of Will? Did you like him?"

"He's a nice guy."

"You don't sound too enthusiastic," Monica said. "I want you all to get to know each other. Give him a chance."

"Definitely," Percy said. "We'll meet up again. Sorry about dinner tonight."

Percy wouldn't mind having dinner with Monica at her apartment, but he didn't want Will to be there.

He didn't think he would like the energy with all three of them in her apartment.

"Maybe Penelope can join us," Percy said.

There was a short pause.

"Penelope?" Monica replied. "Sure. Right. She can join us."

"I should go."

"You should always go, Percy."

He went to the same antique shop that he had gone to the day before. He took the list of names he had found in Macy's bedroom. Reggie was working at the shop when he got there. She didn't see him though. He walked around the store as she was pricing items. He looked at some of the antiques and noticed that some of the things in the store were also on the paper with the list of names, the type of antiques, and the antiques' prices. He had also found another list at Macy's house, which contained a list of antiques, their store price, and then another price was listed next to it. Percy looked at the paper and saw that two wooden-bird figurines were listed there. They were on the shelf. The price next to the item said $85. The price on the actual items was $105. He walked around a bit more and saw a small rug that was also on the list. The price on the list was marked at $800, and the price tagged on the actual rug was $1100. Reggie jumped as Percy called her name.

"Do you remember me from the other day?" he asked.

She looked at Percy for a few seconds.

"So many people come through the store."

"I was here yesterday, wondering about the M.M.C. Remember? I asked you about the initials, but we were never able to finish the conversation. You walked off into the back and never came out again, and then the other guy told me it was closing time."

"I don't know anything about that," she said. "Can I help you look for something? We should be having a new shipment coming in a few days, if you want to wait."

"I have a list of names, under the title of M.M.C. The list belongs to Macy Thorpewaite. Do you recognize any of these names?"

Percy showed her the list. She didn't touch the paper, but looked at the names, as he held the paper in front of her. She lowered her eyebrows.

"I don't recognize any of those people," she said. "Why do you have this? Seems awkward going around asking people if they know anyone on a list of random names."

"I don't think they're random—that's the thing. Did you know Macy?"

Reggie was starting to get agitated. Percy could tell that she really didn't want to talk to him and that she was uncomfortable.

"What exactly do you want?" she asked. "I'm trying to work here. I can't just stand around and play twenty questions with strangers."

Percy was aggravated with her just as much as she was annoyed with him. It wouldn't have to be twenty questions if she would just answer my queries, he thought. He thought about Penelope and her bra.

"Macy had a paper with a list of names, including your name. Eventually, you're going to have to answer some questions, either from me or the police. All I want to know is what do the initials M.M.C. mean?"

"So who are you?" she asked.

She was stalling, delaying, doing anything she could to avoid his questions. She started to walk away, but Percy followed her.

"I was Macy's neighbor, and I also used to work for her."

She looked around the store. There was no one else around. She walked to the front of the store and locked the entrance door. She flipped the Open sign to the Closed For Lunch sign. She told Percy to follow her into the back area of the store, where only the employees were allowed. They entered her office. She sat in the chair behind her desk, and Percy sat in a chair opposite to her. On the desk, there was a black bag which looked familiar to him, but he couldn't quite remember where he had seen it before.

"I can't tell you much," she said.

"That's fine, but tell me as much as you can for now."

"I shouldn't be telling you anything. It's none of your business in the first place."

"If you could be kind enough," Percy said. "I feel like it's my business, in a sense, because Macy has left me all of her estate."

"All of it?" Reggie replied.

She looked like she knew something—that Percy actually didn't inherit all of Macy's estate.

He sneezed. Reggie handed him a tissue.

"There is no police involvement?" she asked.

"Not yet. But they are searching for any leads to find the burglars, and if I have to go to them to find out what I need to find out, I will. And that would mean that they would come to you because I'll mention your name."

Bluffing.

"It all has to do with underground antique auctioning," she said.

Percy didn't understand what she meant. He looked at the bag on the table again.

"There are a lot of us. We have exclusive antique auctions."

"Why so secretive about it?"

"Because it involves stolen things. That's why it's underground."

"How long has this been going on?" Percy asked.

"I'm not sure. I've been a part of it for about three or four years now, though."

"How does it all work?"

"I can't tell you that. I took an oath. I shouldn't have even told you what I have just said. You should go now."

Reggie stood up. She appeared nervous to Percy, as if she was about to get in trouble.

"What about the initials M.M.C.?" Percy asked.

"That's all I can tell you. Please go now," she said.

Percy stood up and thanked her. He told her that he might be back if he had any more questions. She told him she wouldn't answer any more questions. He walked to the door of the office that led to the main area of the store.

"You know her funeral is tomorrow?" Reggie asked.

"Whose?"

"Macy's."

"I knew about it. How do you know about it?"

Percy lied. He didn't know that there was going to be a funeral. He didn't try to plan one himself because he thought that he would be the only one there. He didn't think she knew too many other people. Reggie said it was in the newspaper.

"She really cared for you," Reggie said.

As Percy left, he realized that there was so much going on that he didn't know about. Underground auctioning with stolen items? Was Macy a thief who took part in this? How does one become a part of this organization? It was still bothering him that he didn't know what the initials M.M.C. meant.

"What have you been up to, Macy," Percy said. "What is this all about? I wish you would've told me. I can keep secrets."

He tried calling Penelope a few times during the rest of the day to give her an update, but he couldn't reach her. The last time he tried, her friend, with whom she was staying, picked up the phone.

"Is Penelope there?"

"Is this Percy?"

"Hi, I'm Percy."

Penelope's friend introduced himself as Tyler.

"I actually haven't seen Penelope in a while. I figured that maybe she was staying at your place."

"Do you think she's okay? Did the M.M.C. kidnap her?"

"The M.M.C.? She just goes off on her own from time to time. Sometimes she just needs her space. I'm sure she'll be back soon. I'll let her know you called."

Percy was getting worried about Penelope just like he would get worried about Macy when she would be gone for extended periods of time. Perhaps, she was on a lead, too, Percy thought.

43

Percy was surprised by the number of people who were at the funeral. He didn't recognize anyone. He didn't remember Macy ever talking about anyone else except her childhood friends. After the funeral service, there was a small reception. He stayed for a bit to see if he could get any new information. Everyone knew everyone. People were talking and laughing. There was a large display of food which consisted of everything from fried chicken to spaghetti to tiny sandwiches. Percy approached an older-looking man who was pouring himself a glass of water. Percy said hello and introduced himself. The man looked about the same age as Macy. He wore a black suit with a red tie. His bushy gray eyebrows matched his unkempt hair.

"How did you know Macy?" Percy asked.

"How did you know Macy?" the man asked.

"I was her neighbor, and I also worked for her."

"You worked for her?"

Percy nodded.

"That's odd. I've never seen you around before. I used to work for her as well."

"She was a great lady," Percy said.

"She sure was."

His name was Kyle Barret. He didn't tell Percy what kind of work he did for Macy, and they ended up talking about the Atlanta Braves. Percy didn't know anything about baseball, but he was able to keep up the conversation.

"Jones is finally back," Kyle said. "How about that?"

"Good old Jones," Percy said.

He didn't know who he was, but he guessed that he was a good baseball player for the Braves.

"Maybe now we could get a few more wins," Percy said.

"The pitching could be a lot better," Kyle said.

"Tell me about it."

Percy realized that he wasn't going to get any more information from Kyle. They were too deep into a discussion about baseball. He could tell he didn't want to talk about anything else. As he said bye and walked away, Kyle tapped him on the shoulder.

"I'll see you soon," he said.

"Soon?"

"The next session will be held this week. You didn't know."

"I completely forgot," Percy said. "I guess my mind was all wrapped up with Macy."

"I understand."

"Is it at the same place?" Percy asked.

"Yes. It has been a while since we've had one. But it'll be a nice way to say bye to Macy. A different kind of funeral service."

Percy scratched his head.

"Remind me again, where's it going to be?"

"Under the ground," he said. "I'm not working this round. I guess you're also off then."

"Yeah, no one told me anything, so I guess I don't have to work."

"Lucky man," Kyle said.

He shook Percy's hand and walked to a small group of people talking in the corner of the room. Percy saw Reggie talking to someone as he was getting ready to leave. She saw him and smiled. She finished her conversation and turned to Percy.

"It's underground?" he asked.

She took a sip from her glass and looked around.

"That's where the auctions are held," Reggie said. "You shouldn't be talking about this here. No one should be talking about it."

"Are you going to be there?" he asked.

"Go try the fried chicken. It's really good."

She didn't answer his question but continued to look around the room. After a few seconds, she walked away without saying anything. Percy realized that it might be too difficult to get any information at the funeral. As he started to walk away, he noticed an attractive lady in a black dress standing in the corner. He gave her another look, Penelope. His eyes lit up in excitement and walked toward her. He almost shouted her name.

"Penelope," he said. "It's me, Percy."

She looked startled at first and then smiled.

"Hey stranger."

"I've been wondering where you've been. I even talked to your friend, Tyler."

"I was just taking a break from reality," Penelope said. "And then I found out about Macy's funeral today and thought I'd come and see if I can find out some more information."

"Same here," Percy said.

Penelope looked nervous to Percy, like she didn't want to be noticed, or that she didn't want to talk to him.

"Is everything okay?" Percy said.

Penelope shook her head.

"I'm fine. Did you find out anything?"

She looked at Reggie as she was at the food table. Reggie looked back at her.

"Do you know her?" Percy asked. "Her name is Reggie. She works at an antique store. That's why I wanted to get in touch with you. I think she knows what M.M.C. means."

"I don't know her. I was just looking at her because she was looking at you."

Percy told her what he found out through Reggie—that there was an underground auctioning group involving stolen items.

"I think Macy was a part of it," Percy said.

"Interesting. We may have to press her a bit to get more information."

Penelope didn't sound interested or excited about the information. Percy started to feel bad—he thought that he was annoying Penelope instead of fascinating her with the new lead.

"I'll let you go," Percy said.

He put his head down.

"I'm sorry for bothering you."

As he started to walk away, Penelope put her hand on his shoulder.

"No, wait, Percy. I'm sorry. I'm just exhausted. Maybe we should take a break from all of this M.M.C. search and lay low for a while."

"Maybe," Percy said. "But I want to give it a bit more attention before taking a break. I understand if you don't want to, though."

"I just don't want you to get in trouble or hurt."

"Hurt," Percy said.

He looked at the people at the reception—they all seemed to be in good spirits, eating and laughing.

"I didn't realize Macy knew so many people," Percy said.

"It looks like she was well loved and respected."

"I'll go now. Maybe we can meet up some time later on?"

Penelope looked around the room, as if she was searching for someone.

"Definitely," she said. "Be careful, Percy."

44

MACY THORPEWAITE
1925-2008

Macy Thorpewaite lived a life full of muumuus. She brought bright colors to those around her, revealing to them the secrets of fun and anticipation.

45

He woke up the next morning as the phone was ringing. He let the answering machine pick it up.

"It's Monica—just calling to see how you are doing. Work has slowed down a bit, so give me a call. Oh yeah, before I go, Will and I were going to watch a movie tonight, probably around nine. Give me a call before then. Bye-bye."

Percy didn't want to go see the movie with Monica and Will. He just wanted to spend time with Monica, and Monica only. He wasn't sure if he was going to call her yet. He called Allen and they decided to meet for lunch in fifteen minutes at The Sea where Allen had tried to make a pass at Percy the last time they had dinner.

Allen was already at the restaurant when he arrived. He sat at the same table at which they had dined the last time they ate together. He was talking to the same waiter—Joe. They were getting along fine when Percy sat down. Allen looked happy and well kempt.

He ordered an iced tea. Joe looked at Allen, and they both laughed before the waiter walked away.

"In case you can't tell, we're back together again," Allen said.

"I wasn't quite sure if you were ever together before," he said.

Allen said that they had dated for almost a year before they broke up over irreconcilable differences.

"But things have been a lot better," he said. "We've both grown. Or rather, I needed to do the growing up. He has been great all this time—it just took me time to realize it."

Percy told him what he had been doing the past few weeks, in regards to Macy, and the initials, M.M.C.

"M.M.C.?" Allen said. "I have no clue."

"I just can't picture Macy being a part of anything illegal."

"You can never tell," Allen said. "My mother was a very sweet, and gentle person. She worked as a preschool teacher. And I didn't find out until after her death that she was a cocaine addict."

"Wow."

"I took it pretty badly. She died of a drug overdose. It was in the newspaper, front page. She was linked to a politician. So what are you going to do about this antique auction coming up?"

"I need to figure out where and when it is. It should be coming up this week. I have a possible source at one of the antique stores who might tell me something."

"A source? Are you a detective or some kind of news reporter?"

"I'm just a curious guy."

Percy told him how he had become close friends with Penelope—that she made him feel life in a different way.

"I get really nervous when I see her, and my heart starts to breathe fast," Percy said.

"I know that feeling very well," Allen replied.

He looked at Joe taking an order at another table.

"It means you really like her. That you see something special in her."

"Special," Percy said.

Percy continued talking about Penelope, saying how she had been helping him. He also brought up how Monica gave him his mother's contact information. Allen gave Percy all of his attention as he was trying to think things through as far as getting in touch with her.

"What do you think I should do?" Percy asked.

"I think you should be patient and let your thoughts out before you make a decision. Either way, you'll do what you feel like is the best thing to do."

Percy saw Allen as a confident man for the first time. He realized that being back with Joe had completely changed him. He liked the new Allen. Allen changed subjects and asked Percy about his job situation.

"So what are you going to do about money nowadays? You worked for Macy didn't you?"

"Right," Percy said. "I've got a few ideas. I've saved a lot of money. Macy paid me well. She paid me over the amount I should have made. But for now, I'm moving into her old house—she left it for me. I'm going to try my best to keep it. She also left me a lot of money."

"I'll always keep an eye out at the university for you."

Percy also told Allen his idea about the boudin café.

"I'll be your first customer," Allen said.

He sounded excited.

"And maybe I can provide the artwork for the interior."

Percy liked the idea.

"Boudin," he said.

They didn't have to pay for dinner thanks to Joe. Percy thanked them and left while Allen stayed in the restaurant to chat with Joe. Percy went to the antique store where Reggie worked. She saw him as he entered the store. She didn't retreat to the back where he couldn't reach her, but smiled and walked toward him. She was more accepting of Percy this time around.

"Just a few more questions," Percy said.

"I'm not sure if I'll be able to answer them," she said. "But go ahead."

"Where is the underground place? And when is the exact date of the next auction?"

"You were her neighbor, right?" she asked. "It's very close to where you live. Macy's house is just a door."

"I don't understand."

"That's all I can tell you," Reggie said.

"When is it?"

"Tomorrow night, at midnight. That's all I can tell you."

He had a day to figure out where the underground lounge was located. He looked around the store and noticed that a few items were missing.

"What happened to the owl figurines?"

She looked at the shelf.

"I guess someone bought them."

"Did you see who bought them?"

"It may have been sold by the other employee here."

"And the blue and green plates?" Percy asked.

"I guess someone bought those as well," Reggie said.

"So nothing was stolen?" Percy asked.

Reggie looked around the room.

"Not that I know of," she said.

"Looks like business has been going pretty well the past few days."

She didn't say anything and walked to the back of the store where the office was located. As Percy followed her, Reggie turned around and smiled.

"Maybe I'll see you around," she said.

She closed the door on him.

He went back to Macy's house. It was full of boxes as he was still in the middle of moving from the apartment to the house. As Percy packed her items, he found more things with the initials M.M.C. on them. He thought about what Reggie said—what did that mean—the house is just a door? The initials were only on her antiques and on nothing else. He went to the apartment to check the answering machine. He was checking to see if Monica had called. She had left a message wondering if he wanted to see the movie they were going to watch in a few hours. Percy called her back.

"Are you coming?" she asked.

"I'm tired."

"Tired from what?"

"I guess from too much thinking."

She sighed. Percy could tell she was frustrated.

"How about tomorrow night?" he asked. "Are you free tomorrow night?"

"Maybe. I'll give you a call."

"You've been distant, Percy," Monica said.

"I know. I'm sorry. I'll try better, but I just can't right now."

"Have you been spending a lot of time with Penelope?" she asked.

"Not really. Not with anyone all that much. I saw Allen the other day."

"Don't shut yourself in," Monica said. "Especially now. Keep me a part of your life."

"Life," Percy said.

They hung up on a good note, but Percy could tell that Monica was frustrated. Usually, he would be bothered at the thought of Monica being aggravated or angry with him, but this time, he didn't care—he had Macy on his mind.

He went back to Macy's house. Reggie's words kept ringing in his head: "Macy's house is just a door." He started moving his belongings into Macy's house. He figured he would work from the back of the house to the front. He took out all of his clothes and put them away—some went into a dresser and some went into the closet. Her closet still had some plastic hangers, which Percy used to hang his pants and his two long-sleeved shirts. As Percy bent down to pick up a shirt from one of the boxes, he saw a small panel against the back wall of the closet. The size of the panel looked large enough to crawl through. He continued to hang his clothes. He organized the house for a couple of hours and was able to finish his bedroom, the bathroom, and some of the living room. He was happy with the progress he made and decided to call Monica.

"Are you all still watching the movie?"

"There was a change of plans. I didn't think you were going to come, so we decided to rent a movie and order some takeout food."

"Okay."

"You're welcome to come. We ordered Chinese."

"No, you two have a nice night together," Percy said. "What movie did you rent?"

Monica said it was some kind of romantic comedy. Percy loved that particular genre of movies, more so than action movies or thrillers.

"Sounds fun," Percy said.

"Are you okay, Percy?"

"I'm fine."

"You've been acting unusual lately."

"I don't mean to be."

Percy still hadn't figured out where the place was located. But he thought about the panel against the back wall of Macy's bedroom closet. Then he thought about what Reggie had said, "Macy's house is a door." He went to the bedroom closet and pushed aside the clothes that drooped from the hangers to get to the wooden panel. It barely stood out from the wall since both were colored blue, but there was a small latch. He lifted it, and the panel loosened and cracked open. He pulled the panel door and saw a square hole that was big enough to crawl through. The small hallway was too dark for Percy to see anything, so he went back to the living room to get a flashlight, and before tunneling through the mini-hallway, he called Allen.

"I think I've found it," Percy said.

"Found what?" Allen asked.

"The underground place. I think I've found it."

There was a pause, and Allen realized that Percy was talking about the underground auction.

"What are you going to do?"

"I want to see if I'm right. I think I might be onto something."

"Do you want me to come?" Allen asked.

Percy told him no, and Allen told him to be careful and to call afterward.

"If something happens to me," Percy said, "make sure to tell everyone that I said to take care of themselves."

"Who's everyone?" Allen said.

"Well, you take care of yourself."

After he hung up the phone with Allen, he called Penelope, seeing if she wanted to join him. He called her once, and she didn't answer, and he immediately called her again, and again she didn't answer. He wondered if she had her own leads and was working on them just like him. He looked through the tunnel and imagined Macy crawling through it with a cigarette in her mouth and a drink in her hand. She could probably do it with her eyes closed, Percy thought.

Reggie had said the event would take place at midnight. He had about forty-five minutes till then. He showered and dressed. He didn't know what he was exactly dressing up for, but he wore gray slacks and a white button-up shirt. Percy still didn't know how to correctly tie a tie, but he did the best he could. By the time he had finished getting ready, the time was ten till twelve. He didn't know how long it would take to actually reach the end of the tunnel. He filled a thermos with iced tea and started crawling.

The space was comfortable enough, and the floor of the miniature hallway was carpeted. The area was scented with the same smell Percy got in Macy's house, which was the aroma of musk and potpourri. Did Macy crawl through this hole? At first, he thought that she wouldn't be able to travel through such a small space, but with the carpeted floors, and her toughness, he didn't think it would have been a problem for her. She must have fixed this place the way she wanted it, he thought.

Percy crawled for about five minutes. At that point, he was beginning to think that the path was leading nowhere, and he wondered whether he should continue or turn back. He was breathing hard and his elbows were starting to hurt as well as his knees. How did Macy do this? He kept going. With the flashlight on, he saw a bright red light ahead of him. He continued to crawl and reached the end of the tunnel. The bright red light was attached to a door. It was about the same size as the small panel in Macy's closet.

Percy turned the flashlight off and edged to the end of the miniature hallway. He put his ear against the small door. He didn't hear anyone on the other side. He opened the small square door and peered into a room and saw that no one was in it. There were a few tables and chairs, as well as a miniature bar in the room. The floor was carpeted in a dark orange color. The walls were decorated with Monets and Van Goghs and Rothkos. It looked like a museum, and Percy thought that Allen would love this place. He could hear people moving around and shuffling, and saw that there was another door at the other side of the room. He looked around the room again to make sure there was no one else there. He left his thermos and flashlight in the hallway, and entered the room. He moved behind the miniature bar, ready to hide if necessary. He took a glass from the counter and poured a small glass of wine for himself. I could go for a cigarette, he thought.

He could hear movement on the other side of the wall. As he was about to make his way to the door, someone walked into the room—she wore black pants, a white button-shirt, a black bow tie, and a black vest. She looked like she was a waitress in her upper twenties or lower thirties with shoulder-length black hair. She walked toward the bar. Percy sipped his glass of wine, trying to remain calm.

"Can I help you?" she asked.

"Just needed to clear my throat," Percy said.

"Well, just tell me whatever you need, and I'll bring it to you. It's crowded tonight, and I'm working alone, sorry if you had to wait a long time."

"Not a problem," he said. "So it's pretty crowded tonight?"

"You seem young to be here," she said. "I don't remember seeing you here before. I thought I was the youngest person here. Are you new?"

"I was a friend of Macy's."

"We'll miss her."

She said she had to get back to work, and told him to come get her if he needed anything. Percy thanked her as she walked away with a tray of glasses and liquor. She left the room, and he waited for a few seconds before walking through the same door.

On the other side, there was a short hallway with two doors facing each other. Percy couldn't hear anything in the right room, but he could hear people in the left room. He opened the door on the right—it was lit by a table lamp and was full of shelves and tables. They all held antiques, which looked far more exquisite than the ones he had seen in the antique stores. The reflected light from some of the items made the room look like one of those dance clubs with glitter balls hanging from the ceilings. It looked magical to Percy. He walked around the room and looked at the gold and silver plates, bronze figurines, paintings with wooden frames, mantle clocks, and pieces of furniture, such as love seats, sofas, armoires, and ottomans. Every item had the initials M.M.C. There was a small door on the other side of the room. He opened it and found another miniature hallway. It was the same size as the path from Macy's closet. Percy crawled through it wishing he had not left the flashlight behind in the other pathway. It didn't take him as long to reach the end of this corridor as it did from Macy's house to the mini-bar room. The small door at the end of this hallway was on the ceiling of the tunnel.

He opened it and found himself looking at a huge backyard. There was a swimming pool, a Jacuzzi, and a small building that Percy guessed was a guest room, or a changing room. There were multiple gardens, a mini-playground, a patio, and a small waterfall that led to the swimming pool. Greenery everywhere. He climbed out of the hole and ran to the fence where there was a gate leading to the front of the house. The facade of the house looked familiar—he looked at the mailbox. The Wrights. Leo and Jennifer walked out the front door.

"Hello everyone," Percy said.

"What are you doing here at this time of night?" Leo asked.

Percy had forgotten that it was pretty late.

"I think I've figured out some things. I was going to tell you all something, but I just need to find out a little more information."

"Did you find the vase?" Leo asked.

"Not yet. But I may have some leads."

"Then why are you here?" Jennifer said.

Percy told them that as he was going for a walk, he noticed how beautiful their house was, and that he was taking a closer look at it. Percy asked them if he could take a look at the back yard.

"Go ahead," Leo said. "The gate should be open. We're going for a late walk to clear our minds. It has been so stressful lately. Make sure to lock the gate when you leave."

"I'll give you a call soon enough."

They went for their walk, and Percy went into their back yard. He wondered if the Wrights knew about the underground entrance in their back yard. It was hidden behind one of the gardens right next to the fence. The small door was covered in grass. It looked like the fake grass that some football stadiums use. He went back through the hole, through the underground hallway, and returned to the room of antiques. Now it was the other door's turn—the door on the left side of the hallway. Percy walked inside—it was dimly lit. Ahead of him was an elevated stage. Just before the stage were rows and columns of chairs where people sat. No one turned around as he entered, and he sat in one of the chairs in the back row.

On the stage was a table with a wooden stool on top of it, lit by a sparkling chandelier hanging above it. Percy sensed a mystical aura surrounding the stage as if it was the place of utmost importance. He peered over the lady who was sitting in the row in front of him; she was looking at a pamphlet of some sort. There was also a lady standing on the stage next to the wooden stool. She wore a dark purple muumuu. No one was talking. Everyone had a pamphlet in their hands. Percy looked at the door he had entered through and noticed there was a small table next to it with the pamphlets on it. He leaned over and picked one up.

The booklet contained a list of all the antiques, which he guessed were to be auctioned that night. The cover of the booklet read: GOODBYE MACY. He looked around the lounge and recognized some of the people who were at Macy's funeral. On the front page of the booklet was a short list of people who were to speak about Macy. Percy's eyes widened as he saw one of the names. Penelope. He re-read her name at least fifteen times to make sure he was correct. Maybe she found a way in, Percy thought.

"Muumuu," one lady said.

The voice came from the front row. She was sitting on the left side of the aisle. All Percy could make out was that she wore glasses and a muumuu. He looked around and realized that everyone was wearing muumuus. He had to look at one man twice to make sure he was actually seeing what he was seeing. Percy was worried that he would stand out from the rest because he wasn't wearing a muumuu. He looked to see if he could find Penelope, but the crowd was too large, and he couldn't quite see who was sitting at the other end of the room.

After the lady said muumuu, there were a few minutes of silence.

"Muumuu," a man said.

The lady at the stage pointed to him. He gave a large sigh. After a few more minutes, the stool was taken away. From what Percy understood, saying muumuu signified that someone was interested in the item underneath the chandelier. And the last person to say muumuu was the person who got the antique on display. It was their way of bidding.

The next item was a small white horse. Percy looked at the pamphlet and written next to the item was the starting bid, which was a thousand dollars. The guy sitting directly in front of Percy muumuued. No one was looking at each other. No one talked to each other. They all faced forward, toward the stage. It was like they were all in a daze or hypnotized. Percy was the only one turning his head. Another person also made the same noise to let the lady on the stage know that she was interested in the white horse. The guy in front of Percy waited for about thirty seconds until he muumuued again. He grunted out of aggravation. The lady didn't respond, and after a few more seconds, the master of ceremonies pointed to the man in the back. No one looked at him—no one said anything. The man sighed. Everyone stood up, almost simultaneously, and started walking toward the back. They went through the door. Percy looked at the pamphlet and read that after the bidding of the horse figurine there was to be an intermission followed by more bidding and speeches dedicated to Macy. He saw Reggie standing on the stage, and he waited for the people to leave before he went up to her.

"You were able to find the place," she said.

Percy nodded.

"This is a bit strange."

He looked around.

"Do you know Penelope?"

"I do. She's somewhere around here. Nice person."

Percy was wondering if she was able to infiltrate the system or it there was something else going on.

"How do you know her?" Percy asked.

"Ask her. I saw you two talking at the funeral. How do you two know each other?"

Percy told her that she was Macy's niece and she came to town when she heard that Macy had passed away.

"She definitely reminds me of Macy," Reggie said. "Did you figure out the initials?"

She was nicer than usual. Percy looked at everyone dressed in their loose, flowing garments.

"The Muumuu Club."

"Right," Reggie said.

The Muumuu Club.

"It was Macy's idea," Reggie said. "The club started years ago when her husband came back from the War. It wasn't as large as this. I think it was mainly Macy, her husband, Ted, and Janet. They had constructed an underground room and a hallway that connected Macy's house to the Wrights' house. Where the Wrights live now, it used to be a very small house years ago. And the same with Macy. But they saved enough money and they were able to rebuild their houses, creating this underground life."

"Do Mr. and Mrs. Wright know about this?"

"No," Reggie said. "And they shouldn't know about this."

"How come?" Percy asked.

"You'll see. You have to make sure that they don't know about this. Macy would've asked you the same."

"So why muumuus?"

"Macy loved them. She liked the comforting feeling that they provide. It provided color to this dark underground world."

She did wear them a lot, he thought.

"And why all the exclusiveness and secrecy?" he asked.

"Some of the things are stolen. Well, all of the things are stolen."

"Like from the store you work at?"

"And also, for tradition's sake. Macy wanted to keep it very secretive for her own reasons. I guess it makes it somewhat of a prestigious thing to be a part of. She was the adventurous type and dreaded being bored."

"A V.I.P. club for antique lovers or something."

"Something like that," Reggie said. "Excuse me, I need to do some work."

"What about the pricing of the items?"

"Take a look at the pamphlet in your hand. It explains it for you. For each item, a muumuu increases the price of the antique. For example, the gentleman who bought the horse ultimately bought it for two thousand dollars. Each declaration for that particular item was an increase of five hundred dollars."

He looked at the pamphlet and saw that next to the price of the horse was $500. Percy walked into a room that was at the back of the stage. The room was full of antiques. There was another man inside the room. He wore an all-black suit with a white shirt, and black shoes. He had brown hair with a matching beard. Like the waitress, he was younger than the rest of the crowd. He saw Percy and walked toward him.

"Are you a filler?" the man asked.

"Excuse me," Percy said.

"Are you a filler? I thought I was the only one here tonight. But you look new."

"I am," Percy said. "But I don't exactly know what to do. I was kind of thrown into it."

"I hear you," he said. "The same thing happened to me months ago, when I first started. What you do is find a seat and place bids. Either the first bid or after anyone else bids. We are not actually bidding to buy the items, but to get others to bid and raise the price of the antiques. But don't overdo it. Make sure you do it just enough to get the others bidding. But don't over-bid. You don't want to bid too high to discourage the real buyers. You want them to continue their efforts to purchase the item."

"So we're kind of like fake bidding."

"Ghost muumuus are more like it," he said. "We'll alternate after every three. After the intermission, I'll do the first three, and you do the next three. The last item, which is the showcase of the whole auction, we don't have to do anything, because the item itself will prompt all the bidding. It was a gift from Macy—she made it known that she wanted it to be auctioned off after she passed away."

Percy looked at the pamphlet to see the last item, but it didn't say. "To Be Announced" was written instead. The man told Percy to look around the room and become familiar with the items. Percy thanked him for his help, walked around for a few minutes, and went back to the room with the miniature bar.

He had never seen a room full of people wearing muumuus. They were all mingling with one another. Men with blue muumuus talked with other men in green or purple muumuus. Women in multi-colored muumuus conversed with each other. It was a social gathering of a kind he had never experienced before.

It looked like one great extravaganza, full of colors, food, and drink.

As he looked around the room to find Reggie, he felt a tap on the back of his shoulder. He turned around and recognized that it was the man that he had talked to during Macy's funeral.

"Hey, we met at the funeral," Kyle said.

"Jones is playing well," Percy replied.

He wore a bright orange muumuu.

"How come you're not dressed?" Kyle asked.

Percy looked down at his pants and fixed his poorly made tie.

"My old one was torn."

"I hear you. I'm putting all my money on the last item. Keeping my fingers crossed. It's supposed to be a gift from Macy before she passed away."

His eyes widened.

"You know what?" the man said. "I have a spare muu in my bag. You can borrow it for the time being, and give it back to me tonight after the auction, or the next time we meet."

"I'll be fine for tonight. I don't want to cause such a bother."

"I'll be right back," Kyle said.

He took off before Percy could say anything else. As he walked off, Reggie and Percy made eye contact. They walked toward each other.

"Staying out of trouble?" she asked.

"How did you become involved in such a thing?"

"I started young. I used to live next to Macy. We became friends and so on. You know how it goes."

"So you lived in the apartment that I used to live in?"

She nodded. Percy wondered why Macy didn't tell him about this or invite him to the club. He would've kept it as a secret just as much as anyone else, he thought.

"I moved out when you moved in."

Neither of them talked for a few seconds.

"She used to talk to me about you. She really wanted you to be a part of all of this. But she was hesitant because she wasn't sure if you would approve. Would you have approved?"

"I don't really know. This is all very new to me and surprising. Some of the things are stolen."

"All of the things," Reggie said.

"I would've kept it a secret," Percy said. "For Macy. My loyalty is toward her."

"She really wanted to tell you. She told me once that she didn't want to ruin you. She saw you as a very sweet and kind person. She thought of you as if you were her son."

"Why steal the items?" Percy asked.

"That's the rush of it. Getting the antiques. It's more fun for me getting the things than actually bidding for them."

"And your connection is working at the antique store."

"You can't tell anyone," Reggie said. "There's too much at stake, and all the burden will be on you if you tell anyone, especially the police. Put your trust in Macy—she trusted you."

Kyle came back with a muumuu. Reggie used his entrance as her way out and walked away.

"It should fit perfectly," he said.

He walked away. Percy held an orange-and-purple muumuu—he didn't want to offend Kyle so he put it on over his clothes. As the man had said, it fit well. The bottom of the muumuu came to the top of his ankles, and the sides were not too tight or too large for his body-width. He wondered what Macy would've had said seeing him in a muumuu: "Looking good, Penelope," Percy thought.

"You seem to be fitting in just fine," the waitress said.

She handed him a napkin with a phone number written on it and walked away. No one had ever done that to Percy. Did she want him to call her? Whose number was it? The lights dimmed and lightened again. Everyone left the bar and walked back to the auction room. The intermission was over. As the room cleared out, Percy saw Penelope standing at the bar, smoking a cigarette and drinking a glass of wine. He wanted to shout her name, full of excitement from seeing her. He walked up to her and tapped her on the back.

"Hey stranger," Penelope said.

"You're here."

"I am. And so are you."

"How did you get into the organization?"

Penelope took the last drag of her cigarette before putting it out. She sighed.

"I just made the right connections?"

"I've been trying to get in touch with you. Did you know that there's a tunnel leading from Macy's house to this place as well as the Wrights' place?"

Percy couldn't stop talking.

"And that most probably Macy was a part of this organization—I think she headed it. All of the items are stolen."

The room became empty except for a few people finishing up their drinks on the other side of the room. Penelope shook her head.

"I can't do this anymore," she said. "I just can't."

Percy felt like he was annoying Penelope again.

"I'm sorry," he said. "I'm just really happy to see you."

"No—it's not that. I have something to tell you."

She lit another cigarette and took a sip of her wine. Percy thought she looked amazing in her blue muumuu—it looked more like an elegant dress on her than a muumuu.

"I've known all along."

"Known what?"

"This. All of this. The M.M.C., Macy's relation to it, the stolen antiques, the Wrights—all of it. I've known about it since I came to Atlanta."

Percy couldn't quite understand.

"I was sent here for this purpose. I was sent here to meet you and see what you knew about M.M.C., and if you'd ever find out. And I've been sent here to take part in this M.M.C. because it's a tribute to Macy."

"You knew?"

Penelope looked like she wanted to cry—Percy couldn't tell if she was feeling bad or if it was the wine making her eyes look watery. Percy felt like he wanted to cry, too—he had this overwhelming feeling starting from the back of his neck and slowly enveloping his head.

"But why not tell me? Why go through all of this? Why would you be so deceptive?"

"I know," Penelope said. "I'll explain later. I just can't right now. The next round of biddings is about to start."

Percy was speechless.

"I'm so sorry," Penelope said.

"So all of this was just fake," Percy said.

Before she could reply, Percy interrupted her.

"You won't have to explain," he said. "I never want to see you again."

Penelope put her hand on his shoulder as he tried to walk away.

"Please," she said. "Don't be mad."

"Go away," Percy said.

Penelope put out her cigarette and gulped down the rest of her wine. As she was about to speak again, Percy started to walk away.

"Percy," Penelope said. "Percy."

Percy kept walking. He stopped and turned around.

"I feel betrayed," Percy said. "You took advantage of me. I never want to talk to you again."

He turned back around, not really knowing where he should go—he found a door, and walked through and stopped. He peered over and saw Penelope walk into the showcase room. Percy leaned his head back against the wall and closed his eyes, trying to figure out what just happened. Was she sent by the M.M.C to make sure I don't figure them out, he wondered. All he could ask himself was why, why, why.

As he entered the auction room, the ghost muumuu was waiting for Percy.

"Remember what I told you," he whispered. "After every three bids. I will go first."

He ushered Percy to a seat and the ghost muumuu sat a couple of rows behind him. Everyone had entered the room and had taken their seats. The chandelier lit up and shone on the next item on the table, which was a lamp. There were a few moments of silence, and then the ghost muumuu who sat a few rows behind Percy began to bid. His muumuu led a person across the aisle from them to muumuu—this led to more bids. After a few more muumuus, the man behind Percy ceased his muumuus, and a lady acquired the item.

The next two items on display were a small bookshelf and a wooden chest. The ghost muumuu gave a couple of bids on each item before others claimed the items. It was then Percy's turn to participate. He looked at the new clothing he had just acquired and the people around him. They all looked at the next antique that was to be auctioned, which was a ceiling fan.

A person in the same row as Percy muumuued for the ceiling fan. Percy waited for a few minutes.

"Muumuu," Percy said.

He looked around and everyone continued to look at the stage. The same man muumuued again. Percy muumuued. That was his last bid for that item. The man made another offer, and Percy remained silent. He was proud and surprised at himself for getting the job done.

Percy did the same for the next two antiques and was successful. He muumuued on each item twice, leading others to increase their offers. He sat there and traded ghost muumuus with the man who sat a few rows behind him. There were a lot of antiques on display, which meant that a lot of money was being made. As others were saying their muumuus, Percy thought about the future. He thought about talking to Reggie after the auction, and asking her for some kind of permanent position in the Muumuu Club. He didn't like the idea that some of the items that were on display were stolen, or all of them. He thought about gradually making his way up in the Club and changing that. Only legal items would be auctioned, and anything stolen would be rejected. He saw himself as becoming the president of the Muumuu Club. He would take trips all over the world in search of antiques from all cultures. The ones he had seen so far were basically American or European. But he wanted to travel to Africa and Asia and bring all kinds of different products that would lead to the highest bids yet. Perhaps, a global underground Muumuu Club could take shape. He wondered what Macy would have thought about his plan. A whole world that was exclusive only to muumuu and antique lovers.

The last item was about to be put on display, but before they started the bid, there were a few people who wanted to make speeches to the M.M.C. about Macy.

The first person, an elderly man with glasses and no hair, was with Macy from the beginning. He showed no emotion as he talked, but he complimented Macy and all that she had done. The next person was an elderly lady, dressed in a bright pink muumuu with orange around the edges. She was lighter in tone and almost came to tears as she talked about Macy and all that she had done for the organization. Next, Penelope came to the stage. Percy immediately frowned, not wanting to listen to her, but he gave her his attention anyway.

"My name is Penelope, and I'm here to pay my respects to my aunt, Macy. She was well loved by many, and the ones she kept close to her, she dearly loved."

Penelope quickly scanned the room and found Percy.

"Some knew her better than others, and she has taken care of so many people throughout the years. She will be missed, and if she was here to see this celebration, she would walk away because she wasn't one for attention. Thank you, Macy—I hope you like this last item for bid."

Penelope walked off the stage—Percy watched her sit down near the side of the elevated structure.

The chandelier lights went out. The room was dark and quiet. They had come to the final part of the auction. Percy wiped the sweat off the palms of his hands with his muumuu. He estimated that the time was around three in the morning. He wasn't tired at all—he could have gone for at least another few hours. Despite his emotions toward Penelope, he was full of adrenaline—he was enjoying this adventure.

The room became bright with red, yellow, orange, green, and blue strobe lights. The rays of lights swirled all across the room swiftly lighting the faces of the bidders. Classical music was coming from the speakers mounted on the walls—surround sound, and the music was becoming louder and louder as the strobe lights moved faster across the room. Then the classical music stopped, the strobe lights were turned off, and the chandelier was lit brighter than usual, which caused everyone to blink their eyes and look at the ground for a few seconds. The chandelier was sparkling and rotating slowly. The crowd stood up—Percy looked at them, with their faces shining, with their mouths opened. The reflection of the strobe lights shone in those who were wearing glasses—all of their faces turning from blue to red to yellow. Percy found it all to be magical.

There it was—the last item of the show. The real purpose of this particular auction was on the table— Macy's gift to her club. It took Percy a while to realize what the item was, because like the chandelier, it too was sparkling and rotating slowly on the table. He had seen it in the newspaper before. And he had heard Macy speak of it before. Percy remembered the look in Barlow's eyes when Barlow talked about how it had belonged to him, and not the Wrights. The Wrights. It was the missing vase. He understood why everyone would want this thing. The vase rotated slowly on a small platform.

"Gorgeous," Percy said.

Then the bidding began.

"Muumuu."

"Muumuu."

"Muumuu."

"Muumuu."

"Muumuu."

"Muumuu."

"Muumuu."

There was a slew of muumuus. One right after another one, almost everyone in the room was bidding for the vase. There was no need for a ghost muumuu. Everyone in unison sat back down and continued to bid. Percy looked across the room and saw Penelope covered in rainbow colors. Her eyes sparkled as she quietly stood there and watched the spectacle unfold. Despite being mad at her, Percy still thought that she looked pretty, especially with the swirling colors. He became disgruntled again when her words echoed in his head, "I've known all along."

Ten minutes later, as the muumuus slowed down, Percy thought about the Wrights. He could understand why they were really worried about getting the vase back. Leo had grown up believing that the vase belonged to his family because his parents never told them the truth. And it was this fact that bothered Percy. Should I tell the Wrights about their missing vase, he asked himself, or should I not worry about it, and let the auction continue to take place, and never tell them? He stood up and walked through one of the side doors. The door led to a hallway, which led to the back area of the stage. Reggie stood in the back and was looking over everything. Percy guessed that she had one of the higher positions in the club.

"You're not going to tell anyone are you?"

"So Macy did steal it."

She nodded. Damn. Barlow was right after all. Percy could still hear the muumuus going on in the background. It reminded him of popcorn.

"Do you think you can get me in on this? You know, like maybe giving me some kind of job."

"Macy was always thinking about hiring you for the M.M.C.," Reggie said.

"Is there room to move up?" he asked.

"If you stay long enough, possibly. Depends on how good you are and if you're able to keep a simple secret."

Percy nodded and waited for her to continue.

"I won't tell anyone," he said. "I would never want to tarnish Macy's legacy even if it consisted of some wrongdoing."

At least she didn't physically hurt anyone, or kill anyone, Percy thought.

"Drop by the store, and maybe we could go somewhere and talk about it," Reggie said. "But keep this in mind, the job would require full commitment. You can't just up and leave because then the secrecy of the Club is at stake."

"Steak," Percy said.

She turned around and continued to oversee the auction. Percy walked back through the hallway to the room with the miniature bar. The waitress was at the bar preparing drinks.

"Needed a break," she said.

"You like working here?"

"It pays extremely well. Good job security."

"I see," Percy said. "Well, guess I'll go back to the auction. I'll talk to you later."

"You've got that number I gave you," she said.

He walked back to the auction room. From what he understood, Reggie would pretty much give him the job. He could also work with the waitress, as well as move up in the organization and make some really good money. But the Wrights were still in his thoughts. He sat back down in his chair. The muumuus had slowed down, and the bids were down to two people. The length between each of their offers was gradually getting longer, reminding Percy again of a popping popcorn bag slowing down after being in the microwave for about three and a half minutes. He looked at the sparkling vase as it rotated on the small platform, and thought about the Wrights, and his future with M.M.C. He thought about what he should do and what Macy would want him to do. For the first time ever, he went against Macy—at least he thought he was going against her. A part of him hoped that she would actually want him to react this way.

He walked toward the stage. He ascended the small set of steps that led to the platform and made his way toward the vase. The muumuus had stopped. He saw Reggie in the back room of the stage. Her eyes were wide open. Percy reached the display table and looked at the vase as it rotated. He picked it up as the jewels, silver, and gold glittered in the chandelier's light. Everyone in the audience stood up.

"Muumuu."

"Muumuu."

"Muumuu."

"Muumuu."

"Muumuu."

Everyone began to muumuu. No one was taking turns. They were all shouting the words at the same time with their arms raised in the air in protest. Percy looked at the side of room where Penelope was still seated. She was the only one not saying anything. With the glints of the strobe lights, Percy thought he saw her smiling at him. She was the only one who didn't look surprised or shocked. Percy looked at Reggie who looked like she was about to cry.

"Stop it, Percy," she shouted. "She trusted you."

He heard footsteps coming from behind him, and he turned around to see the ghost muumuu who he had been helping after the intermission. His right hand grabbed Percy's shoulder, and his left hand was trying to grab the vase. Percy turned his shoulder away, so the man couldn't get hold of the vase. He blocked the man's left hand with his own left hand and took a couple of steps back.

"What do you think you're doing?" the ghost muumuu asked.

"I'm doing the right thing."

He made another lunge for the vase, but Percy moved aside. The ghost muumuu fell on the rotating platform, twirled around for a couple of seconds before the contraption broke, and he fell to the ground. The crowd had stopped shouting their muumuus. Percy saw that some more people were making their way to the steps of the stage. It looked like one big glob of muumuus to Percy. He ran to the back of the stage where Reggie stood. She tried to get in his way, but Percy moved to the side and passed her. She managed to grab his left arm, but Percy kept running, and she had to let go. He looked back and saw Penelope tripping a few people who were running after him.

He was being chased by muumuus. He ran through the hallway, and back into the room where the auction was being held. Everyone was staring at him, but apart from the four of five people who were running after him, no one else tried to stop him. He arrived at the back door of the room where the waitress stood with a smile on her face.

"What would you like to drink?" she asked.

She grabbed Percy by the arm. Percy stopped and looked at her. She kissed him on the cheek and opened the door for him. He was relieved that she was on his side, though he had no clue why she was being so helpful to him. He ran to the room with the miniature bar and dove through the small hole that led back to Macy's closet.

Percy crawled through the small door in the back of Macy's closet and shut the door. He placed some boxes against the back wall of the closet just in case someone would try to enter through the panel. He found some newspapers that he had used for wrapping some things when he moved into Macy's house and wrapped the vase. He filled a suitcase with his clothes and loaded as many boxes as he could into the car and took off.

He knew Reggie would come to his house, but he didn't want to be there when she did. He also knew that they wouldn't go to the police because then they would have to give away their secret about the M.M.C.

Percy drove to Allen's house. He didn't look too happy as he opened the door, but as soon as he recognized that it was Percy, his mood changed

"Can I come in?"

Allen looked inside his house.

"My house isn't clean. But sure. Please come in."

Allen wore small and tight-fitting shorts with a tank top. Joe was sleeping on the couch in the living room.

The TV was on, but muted.

"We fell asleep in the living room while watching TV," Allen said. "Don't mind him. He's a hard sleeper. So why are you here? Is anything wrong?"

"Kind of. Sort of. I just needed a place to stay for a short bit of time while I think of what to do."

"You know you're always welcome here. And I won't even ask any questions. But if you need to talk about it, feel free to let it out."

Percy thanked him, went to the bathroom, and then went outside to smoke a cigarette. Allen was in the kitchen brewing coffee while Joe continued to sleep in the living room. Percy joined Allen in the kitchen.

"Really sorry for waking you up," Percy said.

"I was planning on getting up early anyway. Joe and I were going to have an early morning at the park. You're welcome to come."

"I got it," Percy said.

"Got what?"

"The vase."

"What vase? Oh. The vase. You got it?"

"Can't really say right now. Maybe later. But please don't tell anyone."

"What are you going to do? They're offering a lot of reward money for that thing."

"I know. Still thinking. Do you mind if I crash here for a bit and get some sleep?"

He showed Percy to the guest room. He got into bed and let the events of the past night filter through his brain as he went to sleep.

Percy awoke around two in the afternoon. Neither Allen nor Joe was home. Allen left a note for Percy saying there was some leftover Lebanese food in the refrigerator, and that they would be back some time in the evening. Percy took a shower and left the Lebanese food for them, and made a turkey sandwich for himself.

He got into his car and drove by the house and was surprised to see that there weren't any cars in Macy's driveway. He drove a bit down the road, a block off from his place, and walked back to his apartment, making sure no one was following him.

47

"May I speak to Ms. Lily, please?"

"This is she."

"Hi Ms. Lily. My name is Percy, and I think I'm your son."

"Wait, who?"

"My name is Percy."

There was a heavy silence between the two. Percy was in his apartment. Without thinking, he had taken out the piece of paper that Monica had given him and dialed the number. He was nervous, and his anxiety made him hungry. His heart was beating fast, and he took a deep breath to calm himself down.

"Percy," Ms. Lily said.

"Should I hang up? I understand if you say yes."

Percy could hear her sniffling.

"No, no. Please don't."

There was more silence.

"Hi, Percy."

"Hi."

She asked him how he was doing. Percy said things were somewhat hectic, but his life was just starting to calm down.

"Do you remember me?" Percy asked.

"I do. I do. I'm just speechless."

"Words."

He took another deep breath.

"Well it was nice talking to you. I guess I should go now—I'm waiting for a light bulb to go out so I can fix it."

He scrunched his face, pacing back and forth in his room. He was always walking around when he was on the phone and would stretch the cord for as long as it could go. He thought about Penelope and Monica and the M.M.C.

"Wait," Ms. Lily said. "Please wait."

Another pause.

"Would you like to meet in person?" she asked.

"I don't know," Percy said. "I really don't know."

She gave him the name of a coffee shop.

"I'll be there at eight tonight. If you want to meet me, that'll be great. If you don't, that's perfectly fine. I understand. And maybe if you're up for it at another time, we can try to connect again."

Percy liked her voice—it was soft and sweet, almost shy-ish.

"Thanks," he said.

"I hope to meet you, Percy. This is so surreal. Thank you for calling."

"Thanks."

They hung up, and Percy continued to walk around the room, staring at the floor, and wondering if he should meet his mother. He wanted to call Penelope. He wanted to call Monica. He wanted to call Allen. He needed Macy. But he didn't get in touch with any of them. As he thought about Penelope, he got a sinking feeling, wondering if he would ever talk to her again. He was still trying to let it all settle in.

He wore a brown corduroy jacket, a button-up white shirt, and gray slacks. In one hand, he held a tie, in the other, flowers from Macy's garden. His hair was wet and neatly combed. He realized that he had no clue what Ms. Lily looked like and quickly found an open table in the corner. He surveyed the room, counting seventeen customers sitting down, and four at the counter. It was 8:07 p.m. He saw one lady sitting by herself at the opposite end of the room. She had long brown hair and was wearing jeans and a t-shirt. Taking the flowers and the tie, Percy walked up to her—she didn't notice him as she was reading a book. Percy tapped her on the shoulder.

"Sorry to bother you," he said. "But are you my mother?"

"I'm afraid you have the wrong person," she said. "But you look nice."

"Hi, I'm Percy. Sorry for the mistake."

The lady was kind and said that it wasn't a problem. As he walked back to the corner of the coffee shop, he heard his name being called. He turned around and saw another brown-haired lady sitting by herself. She was wearing a sundress. There was nothing on the table before her except for a to-go cup. Percy walked up to her.

"Are you Percy?"

"Hi, I'm Percy."

She smiled, and Percy saw that her eyes started to water.

"I'm Lily," she said. "Please sit."

"I have flowers," Percy said. "For you."

He sat down and gave her the flowers while placing the tie on the table.

"Lovely," Lily said.

She put them before her face and smelled them.

"They're real flowers," Percy said.

When he looked into her eyes, he felt like he was looking at himself.

"You're my mom?"

"I am."

For the first time, after the longest time, Percy's eyes became soft, round, and watery. He started to quietly cry. Lily did, too.

Percy felt a sense of relief as his tears came out. He didn't care if there were other people around. He was with his mother.

"I don't know how to tie a tie," he said. "Have you ever heard of boudin? Have you tried it?"

"I've heard of it," Lily said. "But I've never tried it. That's a nice tie."

"Do you know how to tie it? I don't."

Lily took the tie and they leaned toward each other. She put his collar up and put the tie around his neck and fixed it.

"Thanks," Percy said.

"You look like a gentleman."

Percy thought about Macy. He went on to talk about boudin and what it consisted of, and how he loved it and wanted to open a boudin café in Atlanta. Lily listened, looking straight into his eyes. After Percy finished talking, there was some silence before Percy spoke again.

"So you're my mom."

"And you're my son."

"How come?"

"I owe you so many apologies," Lily said.

She started to cry again. Percy did, too. He thought about waffles and ice cream to calm himself down. He didn't care that people were looking at them—it felt good to cry. It had been a while, and he had been wanting to cry for the longest time.

"This feels good," Percy said.

"Where should I begin?" Lily asked.

"I guess straight from the beginning."

"I was really young when I became pregnant with you."

"How old?" Percy asked.

"Sixteen."

"Like sixteen years old?"

She nodded.

Percy just realized that all this time he was thinking about connecting with his mother, that he also had a father, too.

"Do I have a dad?"

"Right. I guess you do."

She said that when she became pregnant, her partner had left her, and he moved away with his parents after she made the decision to have Percy and give him to the shelter.

"That was the last time we saw each other or talked to each other. He wasn't my boyfriend. It was just a random night."

She started to tear up again.

"I'm so sorry," she said. "I wish I had a better story for you."

Percy felt bad for her. He didn't mean to make her go through such an emotional story.

"Please don't," he said. "I understand. You were really young. It's okay."

"I was just a teenager," Lily said. "My parents weren't too helpful and when it came down to it, I was basically on my own. I just wanted to give you the best life possible. I was nowhere near being a responsible parent. I could barely take care of myself at the time."

She went on to say that she and her parents hadn't kept in touch since she moved out of their house when she turned eighteen.

"We all didn't know how to act," she said. "And I felt so guilty for giving you away. I'm so sorry."

Percy looked at the line at the counter.

"I regret it all. I don't regret becoming pregnant—I regret giving you away."

Percy was trying to support her. He noticed how young she looked and realized that she was only sixteen years older than him. He made the decision that he wouldn't try to seek out his father. Percy didn't like how he left her all alone and how he didn't keep in touch with her at all. He didn't even want to bring his father up anymore as he talked to his mother.

Lily continued to talk about her teen pregnancy and how she wanted to see how he was doing, to reconnect with him.

"But I didn't know how you would take it," she said. "Or how I would take it. I didn't want to get in the way of the life you were already living without me."

"I'm here now," Percy said. "And I'm glad. I was thinking the same about intruding into your life and getting in the way."

Lily said that she wasn't married and that she didn't have a boyfriend either, nor any more children.

"You may not believe it," she said. "But I'm still trying to get over what I did to you."

Percy's leg was shaking up and down. He put his hand on his knee to keep it from moving so aggressively.

"The flowers are from my friend's garden," Percy said.

He wondered if he should tell her about Macy, but decided against it. He had already made up his mind that he would meet with Lily again, from time to time, and perhaps become friends with her. He planned on telling her about all that had happened at another time. He hoped that she would be up for spending time together. He thought about Monica and Penelope.

"Thank you," Lily said. "They really are colorful. I can't remember if anyone has ever given me flowers before."

"Your name is a flower," Percy said.

"I wasn't quite sure if you were going to come meet me," Lily said. "And to be honest, I didn't expect you to, but I also have something for you."

She pulled out, from her dress pocket, a small toy car and put it on the table. Percy almost started to cry again but was able to hide it with a large smile. He picked up the toy car and moved it around in the air as if the car was flying. He started to laugh.

"My first real toy," he said. "I love it. I absolutely love it. I'll put it on my bedside table."

They sat there at the coffee shop until closing time. They were the last ones to leave as they talked about anything and everything. It was a lot of small talk, but Percy enjoyed it. He was happy with his decision to meet his mother. He found her to be sweet and kind. He thought of her as another friend. The employees started to close down the coffee shop. Percy saw someone mopping the floor.

"Would you be up for meeting up again?" Percy asked.

"I was about to ask the same," Lily replied. "I would love to—maybe we can go out for dinner or lunch next time.

"Food," Percy said.

They had an emotional hug outside of the coffee shop—tears and a long goodbye.

"See you soon," Percy said.

He walked away, holding the toy car. When he got back to the apartment, he went over to his bedside table and put the car right next to a framed photo he had taken while in New Orleans. He thought about calling Penelope as he picked up the phone. He pressed the first button then hung up. He was still trying to figure out how he felt about everything and told himself that he needed more time. Every time he thought about Penelope, he got a sinking feeling. He called Monica. He didn't want to talk to her about anything else aside from his mother—not Penelope, or M.M.C, or Macy, just his mother. Monica picked up the phone, sounding like she hadn't been awake.

"Hi Monica, it's Percy. Was I sleeping?"

He looked at the clock which read 11:24 p.m., which didn't sound too late to him, but he realized that he also didn't have to go to work the next morning.

"Percy, are you okay?"

"Hi Monica."

He started pacing around his room, going as far as the cord would let him.

"I talked to her," Percy said.

"Penelope? Did you ask her out?"

Percy realized that Monica didn't know that he wasn't talking to Penelope for the time being due to the recent events at the underground auction. He hadn't talked to Monica about M.M.C and wasn't sure if he was ever going to tell her.

"Not Penelope."

"Then who?"

Percy didn't respond. He wanted Monica to figure it out, which didn't take too long.

"Your mother?" Monica replied. "Did you talk to your mother?"

"Not only did I talk to her, but I met up with her, too."

"Hold on," Monica said. "Let me go to another room."

He heard some ruffling noises in the background. She didn't want to wake up Will, Percy thought, realizing that they were probably living together. A few second later, he could hear Monica breathing on the phone.

"Should I come over?" she asked. "I know it's late—maybe we can go to the diner and talk about it. It's open twenty-four hours.

Percy was taken aback by Monica's genuine care for him. She was sleeping—she had to work early the next morning, yet she was willing to not worry about that and meet up with him during the middle of the night. He was humbled.

"Let's meet later," Percy said. "At a better time—maybe on a Friday or Saturday when you don't have to worry about work the next day."

Percy was thankful though and expressed his gratitude.

"But how did it go?" Monica asked.

"Emotional," Percy replied.

He continued to pace back and forth.

"But it went great," he said.

He told her the basics of their encounter, saving the details for when he and Monica would meet at a later date. He mentioned their phone conversation and how he and Lily met at the coffee shop, and how she looked. Monica sounded like she was sniffling.

"I am so happy for you," she said. "I love you so much."

Percy stuttered. It was the first time Monica had ever told him that she loved him. He wanted to swallow her words.

"I love you, too, Monica."

48

Penelope had been calling Percy repeatedly. Sometimes, he was at his apartment when she called, but he didn't pick up the phone. When he wasn't at his apartment, Percy would come back to find his answering machine full of messages from her. He wasn't staying at his place, or Macy's house. He was staying at a hotel not too far from where he lived and would go to his apartment randomly, just to hear Penelope's messages. Sometimes he was happy and hopeful—other times, he was angry.

He loved the hotel life—he always found it as a new world and his favorite parts were the tightly fixed bed sheets, the breakfasts, and the feeling of anonymity. He would mainly just sit in the lobby and watch people walk in or out. He had become more accustomed to smoking, coughing less and less, and would sometimes sit outside and watch people and cars pass by. Percy was staying at the hotel because he didn't want to be found by Penelope. He knew not to stay at the hotel where Monica worked because she'd find him there so he found another spot not too far away from his place.

He went back to his apartment to check the latest message from Penelope, which said, "Please call me," and that was it. It was her shortest message so far, and Percy could tell that she was at a loss. He thought about calling Monica but then decided against it, wanting to handle this situation on his own. That latest message from Penelope led to Percy finally giving in. He felt bad as he could hear the sense of despair in her tone. He never wanted anyone he cared about to feel bad.

He checked out of the hotel and moved back into his apartment. He called Penelope. This time, he didn't pace around the room, but rather he sat on the foot of his bed. He still had conflicted emotions, so when he called her, he tried his best to not be himself. Penelope picked up the phone.

"Yes," Percy said.

"Percy?"

"Yes."

"Where have you been? I was worried."

"What did you want?"

Percy realized that he was being somewhat harsh with his tone, but continued to act mean. She's lucky that I'm calling her back, he thought. He felt bad for thinking that—he felt out of place and not himself. Penelope's voice was soft, and Percy could tell that she was feeling bad for all that had happened. He decided to be honest.

"You hurt me," Percy said.

"I know. I don't know what to say. I'm so sorry. I sincerely apologize."

"Why didn't you tell me? What's the point of all of this?"

He stood up and started to pace around. Penelope asked if they could meet in person. Percy thought about Monica and remembered when she told him to be careful because she didn't want him to get hurt. She was right, Percy thought, I ended up getting hurt.

"I don't know," Percy said.

"Please let me explain. I feel horrible, but I had to do it, out of respect for my aunt. Can we, please?"

This raised Percy's curiosity. He paused and then nodded his head. He waited for a few seconds before realizing that Penelope couldn't see him nod his head.

"Okay."

Penelope sounded excited.

"Great," she said. "Thanks."

They decided to meet at the 24-hour diner, the same one they went to after breaking into the antique store. Meeting time was at midnight as Percy wanted to take care of some things at Macy's house before doing anything else.

When he arrived at the diner, only a few people were there. He saw Penelope sitting in the corner of the restaurant. He became excited and wanted to shout her name and wave, but he kept his excitement to himself. He wondered if he should've called Monica to join him, but he knew it was too late for her as she had to go to work in the morning. Penelope's head was down as she stared into her cup of coffee, not noticing Percy walking up to her.

"I'm here," he said.

"So nice to see you."

Percy sat down on the opposite side of her.

"Nice corner spot," he said. "I would've chosen the same table."

"I know," Penelope said.

She held a piece of paper in her hand. Leaning in toward Percy, she took a deep breath.

"I am sorry," she said. "I really didn't want to do this, especially after meeting you. The whole time I felt like I was betraying you, even when I really didn't even know you."

Percy looked into her eyes—they were round and large, watery and beautiful. He could tell that she really meant what she was saying, but he also thought about how he thought that she meant everything she had done and said in the past, and it was all a deception. He gave her the benefit of the doubt and lightened up. He had been angry with her—it was the first time he was truly mad at someone, and he found the emotion unappealing. He didn't want to be mad at her anymore, or ever again.

"What happened?" he asked.

"Before I say anything," she said. "Please know that everything I said, in relation to what I think about you, how I acted around you, that was all so very true. I really do like you."

She sighed. Percy had never seen Penelope so distraught. He felt bad for her.

"Thanks," he said. "That really means a lot."

A waiter walked up and asked if they wanted anything. Percy looked at Penelope who was looking back at him. He ordered an iced tea and waffles with sausage links.

Penelope was glad that he ordered food and she did the same, ordering a chicken fried steak with gravy and a side of mashed potatoes.

"What's that in your hand," Percy asked.

Penelope fiddled with the piece of paper.

"It's for you. But before I give it to you, I just wanted to tell you that she did this all for you. Me, coming here, and trying to figure all of this out with you, she wanted me to do this, and that's why I came to Atlanta—for you."

She gave Percy the piece of paper but told him not to open it just yet.

"Before you read it, just know that she absolutely adored you. Loved you. And all of this, her intentions were to give you an adventure—to give you a break from everyday life."

"With Macy," Percy replied, "every day was an adventure."

Penelope put her hand on his wrist.

"I hope you understand," she said. "And I love you—I really do. I was amazed with you the first time that you peered around the side of the door. You're sweet and handsome."

"Handsome," Percy said. "Sweet."

He looked at her lips and wanted to kiss her. He opened up the folded piece of paper.

"When she passed away," Penelope said, "I received this in the mail—it's broken up into two parts. One for me, and one for you. Read both."

Penelope,

My dear, it has been a while. I hope this letter finds you well, and if you're reading this, it looks like I'm not doing too well. As I'm no longer alive, I have left you some inheritance—please see the attached card for the contact information of my attorney. Please note that most of my estate will go to a young man named Percy (more on him in just a bit).

Penelope, I am so sorry about the rift between your mother and me. Know that no matter how angry we were with each other, that our love for each other was always there, a love that was as strong as love can be. After all, we were twins. And my love for you never ended and I thought about you every day. You don't know this, but I was at your mother's funeral—I hid behind a tree, letting the branches act as my umbrella under the rain, and when I saw you standing next to the coffin, I was in tears. You are quite the adult now, beautiful, and I'm sure you are doing some amazing things with your life. My love for you will grow even more after I'm gone—take care of yourself. As a child, you were always strong and independent—always remember that as you meet the obstacles of life. I love you. I love your mother.

Now on to Percy. Oh mercy me, where do I begin. Percy lives in the apartment above my garage. I have never met anyone like him and I grew fond of him very quickly. He is a sweetheart. He is a gentleman. But he is also very sheltered. While being kind and great and thoughtful, I feel like he needs to experience an adventure. I feel like he needs to feel life. This is where you come in as I'm sure you're up for the task. As you know, the main argument between your mother and me was about The Muumuu Club—she once told me that she told you about it. As I'm now gone, I would like you to help Percy to open up a bit. He may find out about M.M.C. or he may find out a little bit about it and become curious about its meaning—that along with the recent visits of my former friends from back in the day should lead him to be curious. As stated in my testament directed toward you, you will be a part of the next M.M.C to finalize my contribution to the organization (I hope that you will take part). If you do take part in this, find Percy. Guide him. Support him. Steer him. Help him to break barriers and feel both comfortable and uncomfortable with the unknown. Help him to feel new every day.

I would like for him to take part in an adventure so he can break away from the mundane aspects of life. I am very fond of this man—he's the first person, in a long time, who genuinely means to be a good person for no reason at all. He knows no other way of being. When you meet him, you'll see what I mean, and I can foresee a strong relationship between you two. He is a sweet person. Help him,

Penelope—show him the thrilling side of life. Please see the attached sheet for contact information in regards to M.M.C. I end this portion of the letter to you. Keep growing, keep seeking.

Love,
M.T.

Percy finished the first part of the letter and looked up at Penelope.

"I know," Penelope said.

She took Percy's hand and kissed his wrist.

"I miss her," Percy said.

"I know. I hope that you're understanding a bit more."

As he was reading the letter, he didn't realize the waiter had brought their food to the table. He saw his plate and Penelope's—she hadn't touched her meal as she was patiently watching Percy read.

"Should we eat?" he asked.

"Let's wait until after."

Percy tapped Penelope's wrist and then went on to reading the rest of the letter which was specifically directed to him.

Dear Percy (my little Penelope),

I'm sorry to have left you like this, on your own. However, I know that you are more than capable of carrying on without me. I admire you and respect you, Percy. Why? Because you honestly care. You want to be good. You are good. You have opened me up to a whole new world. Thank you for that. And now, I'm trying to reciprocate.

I'm assuming by now that you've learned about the other life I had been living, if not finding out everything about me. I really am sorry, and I hope I didn't lose your respect. Please know that I didn't do this just for the money—for all profits went to various organizations, including shelters and so on. I did it for that reason and also for the reason of just simply being bored—I needed activity, I needed excitement. The older I became, the more I felt suffocated, trapped in a mundane life, especially after Zephyr's passing. I needed an adventure or rather, I needed adventures and so came the birth of M.M.C.

I wanted you to have an adventure, too.

And that's why I asked Penelope for her help. Please don't be mad at her, at least give her a second chance if you did get mad at her. If anything, just be mad at me. She was just doing what I asked her to do, and we both meant well as we wanted you to experience an adventure and take a break from the normalcy of life. I hope you don't mind. I'm sure you have found Penelope to be a sweet and loving person, much like her mother.

I'm not sure what else to write, Percy. I hope you're doing well with all of this, and most importantly, I hope you had an adventure.

With Love,
M.T.

Percy finished reading the letter but continued to stare at the piece of paper, reading various lines over and over again. He looked up at Penelope.

"I miss her so much."

"I know."

"I'm not mad anymore," Percy said. "I now understand."

"Thanks, Percy."

"Thanks."

"I was just being true to you in several other ways ever since I met you. I find you absolutely adorable and sweet. You are a gentleman."

"Can I hug you?"

Penelope shifted over to Percy and hugged him—it was a long embrace, each of their heads on each other's shoulder. They let go, but Penelope didn't move back to her seat. She remained close to Percy. He could feel the warmth of her breath upon his face. Penelope gave a deep sigh. Percy noticed that she was still looking sad.

"I'm leaving tomorrow, Percy."

"Are you going to the zoo?"

"I'm going back to Chicago."

Percy looked down at the surface of the table. He couldn't look at her. He knew this time would eventually come but was hoping for it to happen later, if not never. Penelope took out a pen and grabbed a napkin.

"This is my contact information in Chicago. I promise you I'll come visit. But I would love it if you'd come up to Chicago some time. Please do."

She pushed the napkin toward Percy.

He hadn't told anyone, but Percy was going to leave Atlanta for a while, too, as he had decided to go down to New Orleans soon for a getaway. He picked up the napkin and neatly folded it before putting it in his wallet.

"Do you think we'll ever see each other again?"

"I promise."

The thought of not seeing her gave him a feeling of loss and despair. Penelope reassured him and promised again.

Both of them realized that they hadn't touched their food and started to eat. They ate silently, not saying a word to each other, and when they finished, and after Penelope paid for both of them, Percy put his head against Penelope's head and whispered into her ear.

"I will visit you and maybe we can get some hot dogs."

He paused.

"With relish."

Penelope closed her eyes and whispered into Percy's ear.

"I believe you."

They sat there together, talking well into early morning. The sun was rising, and when it was time to go, they kept their goodbyes simple. Penelope gave Percy a light punch on his shoulder.

"I'll see you soon," she said.

"See," Percy said.

49

Percy went to the hotel to see if he could find Monica. He had a lot of thoughts brewing in his head, and for some reason he wanted to see Monica. He had made the decision that he was going to leave Atlanta—maybe not permanently, but definitely for the time being. He wanted to say bye to her, and he wanted to wish her luck with Will and her job. He had already said bye to Penelope and had already thought about visiting her in Chicago soon.

Percy found the hallway that Monica usually walked through whenever she was going to her office. He looked at the doors for the nametags and came to Monica's door. He tapped on the door.

"Come in," she said.

Percy opened the door and saw her sitting at her desk. She looked professional with her papers neatly organized in stacks on her desk. She had a couple of shelves with large hardback books. On the walls were pictures of her family, as well as one with them in New Orleans. Percy remembered when and where they took that picture.

"It's one of my favorites," she said.

She pulled out a yo-yo from her drawer and tossed it to Percy.

"I use this whenever I need to think," she said. "I think it's very unprofessional."

"These things are more complicated than they seem."

He tried to yo-yo, but he didn't flick his wrist quick enough, and the yo-yo hit the floor. He wound it up and gave it back to Monica, but she told him that he needed to keep it.

"Practice," she said. "There's a tournament coming up soon. And I want you in it."

Percy walked behind the desk, bent down, and gave her a hug. She put her arm around his back.

"Are you okay?" she asked.

"I'm just going to take off for a while. And I wanted to see you one last time before I left."

"Are you in trouble?" she asked.

"Not exactly," Percy said.

"Well then, what is it?"

"I just need to get out for a bit."

"Is it because of your mother?" Monica asked.

"Not at all. I'm so glad to have met her. We'll meet again soon."

"Is it because of Penelope?"

Percy wondered if he should tell her about Penelope, but decided not to—everything was fine between them, and telling Monica might get her angry even though he and Penelope had already reconnected.

"Everything is fine with Penelope," Percy said. "I really like her. She left for Chicago."

"Do you think you all will keep in touch?"

Percy fiddled with the yo-yo, dropping it on the floor. He didn't answer her. Before he left, he gave her Allen's phone number and told her that if she ever needed any help to give him a call.

Percy glanced at the door directly across from her office, and the tag on the door read Will Saccron.

"Make sure he treats you right."

"Who?"

Percy walked away, but as he was about to exit the hotel door, he felt his hand clasped by another hand—a soft touch. He looked to see who had grabbed his hand and saw Monica, who kept walking, leading him out through the doors.

"Hi, Monica," Percy said.

"Come on," she said.

She didn't speak after that, but continued to hold his hand—they walked down a few blocks until they came to a bar. They walked in and sat at the counter. She still hadn't spoken.

"How are we doing," Percy said.

She didn't reply. She ordered two shots and handed one to Percy. She clinked her glass against Percy's and swallowed her shot. Percy, not sure what was going on, did the same—causing him to cough and his eyes to become red and watery. Once he was able to compose himself, he opened his mouth to speak, but Monica put her hands on each side of his face and kissed him on the lips—a long kiss. When they finished, Monica pulled her head back—her hands still on each side of Percy's face. He looked lost as he stared at Monica's chin. He found a way to talk.

"How are we," Percy said.

"Please don't do this."

Her voice was soft and comforting to Percy.

"How are you doing," he said.

"You know," she said. "The main reason why I looked for a job here was because of you."

Percy didn't know what to say. Monica ordered a drink for each of them.

"When I moved away, there wasn't one day I didn't think about you, hoping that you're doing well."

"I like to garden," Percy said.

"And when I came back and started meeting up with you again, all I could do was think about those wonderful memories we had together."

Percy sipped his drink, reminding him of Macy sitting on the porch.

"I don't know how to say this," Macy said.

"You just became my first kiss," Percy said.

Monica continued to talk.

"I was in love with you," she said. "You were my first love. But I didn't want to tell you because I didn't want to ruin the great friendship we had. That was more cherishing than any other feeling."

"I always wanted to hold your hand," Percy said.

"And I met Will," she said. "And he's a great guy, and we will get married most probably and have children and so on, but just know that no one will ever compare to the bond that we had."

"What do I do?" Percy asked.

"Find someone," she said. "And let her love you."

"Penelope."

"Yes, Penelope, if she's the one. Go for it. Live and feel life. Love."

They both took a sip and stared at the counter.

"The first time I learned about love was reading a book called *The Giving Tree* while I was in the shelter."

"Tell me about it," Monica said.

Percy went on to talk about his past thoughts and feeling, most of which he had never talked about before.

Monica listened with great interest, constantly looking into his eyes. Her own eyes were watery and round. Percy went on to describe every page of the book.

"It always reminds me of the other children and our guides at the shelter," he said. "And how we were always looking after each other."

He took another sip.

"Oh," Monica said. "Tell more about your visit with your mother."

Percy smiled. He started talking and couldn't stop as he gave her the details about their time spent at the coffee shop.

"I think she's great," Percy said. "I'll get in touch with her again soon."

"And now you're saying that you're going away," Monica said.

"New Orleans for now," Percy said.

"For good?" Monica asked. "Please come back. Let's continue our friendship. Let's grow together."

Percy's voice was confident and strong.

"I promise you I'll be back, and we can eat crêpes together."

"Lovely," Monica said.

They hugged and finished the last of their drinks. They held hands as they left the bar—outside, they hugged again without saying a word, and as they parted ways, Percy called Monica's name. She turned around.

"Otters," he said.

"The cutest ever," Monica said.

"I promise," he said.

"Crêpes."

And as they walked away, Percy thought about the future, loving the idea that when he would return, there would be a friend here, waiting for him.

Allen and Joe weren't home when Percy got back, which was the way he wanted it. He left Allen a goodbye note. He thanked Allen for his help and for being such a good friend. He also wrote that he would give Allen a call later and explain everything to him about the vase. He ended up writing more than he thought he would. He made his bed, which he had forgotten to do earlier. As a good-bye gift, he left Allen the afghan that Macy had given him. He wrote in the note that Allen should hang it on the wall rather than use it as an actual blanket.

Percy drove to the Wrights' house. There were a couple of cars in the driveway so he figured someone was home. He rang the doorbell, and a few seconds later, Jennifer opened the door. They went through a large living room and sat in a smaller room that was adjacent to it. Jennifer wore khaki pants with a red button-up shirt. Her blond hair was tied into a ponytail. She told Percy that Leo was still at work but that he should be home within the next couple of hours. Percy told her that he didn't plan on staying that long.

"Any news on the vase?" she asked.

"Not really, but I think I may know where it could be, but I don't want to get any hopes high, or start any rumors."

She sighed.

"You all really love this vase," Percy said.

"It has become a large part of our family."

She started talking about raising the reward money. Percy didn't know why he didn't give her the vase right then. He wasn't really interested in the reward. He was more interested in how the Wrights really loved the vase. It wasn't a prize possession for them like it was for Macy or the Muumuu Club. They honestly loved the item for what it represented, which was more of a family thing. He thanked Jennifer for her company and told her that he would give them a call later on. She was also leaving the house to do some errands.

Percy backed out first and made a loop around the block as he waited for Jennifer to leave, and then he drove back to their house. He took the vase out from one of the boxes in his car—he gave it one last look and went to the porch and placed the vase against the door of the house. He got back into the car and made his way to the highway. He was going to New Orleans.

50

Allen,

Thank you for your help. Thank you for getting me to the hospital, and thank you for visiting me in the hospital—I don't have too many friends, and it really meant a lot. It also meant a lot that you let me stay over when I needed a place to sleep.

I'll call you later to explain everything—once everything has cleared up. I'm leaving you an afghan. Don't use it as a blanket—it looks better on the wall, just a thought.

I'm off to New Orleans, and from there, who knows? I have this craving to see Oprah, so maybe I'll venture off to Chicago. I've given my friend, Monica, your phone number. She is a friend of mine, and in case she needs help with anything, I told her to call you. I hope that's okay.

What else, what else. Oh, sorry that I'm not gay. And I hope I didn't hurt your feelings or anything—it's just the way things go. You're a great guy, and I think if I were gay, I would totally be into you. Well, it's actually good that it didn't work out, because now you and Joe are back together, and I won't have to worry about being in the way.

Anyway, take care of yourself. Maybe I'll come back some day and see if there is another job opening at the university. Also, from time to time, drive by Macy's house to make sure it's still standing or whatever. If you want, you can stay there too.

Later,
P. Winks

51

Percy checked in at the same hotel that he had stayed in with Bill and Monica when they had all gone to New Orleans together. He got there around three in the morning, but he wasn't tired—he was more excited than anything else.

He walked to a nearby café—it was still open. There were a few people in there, and the stage was set with instruments, but no one was playing. He ordered a coffee and lit a cigarette. A man at the table next to him asked for a light. He wore a white t-shirt with brown pants and black dress shoes. He wore one of those old hats, similar to the ones horse jockeys wore.

"What brings you here?" he asked.

His voice was scratchy.

"Jazz," Percy said.

"Well," he said. "Let's see what we can do for you. Thanks for the light."

He walked over to the bar where there were two other people sitting. They wore similar clothes as well. The man who had talked to Percy pointed toward him and they took a shot and stood up—they made their way to the stage and picked up the instruments. After a few seconds of tuning, they began to play. Percy ordered a beignet and another cup of coffee and watched them play till early morning. The morning crowd started to come in to get their breakfast, and that was when they stopped playing music. It was around six-thirty in the morning.

"Well how about that," the man with the blood-shot eyes said.

"I want to eat your music," Percy said.

He bought their CD and went back to his room at the hotel. He tried to sleep, but it didn't last too long. Once he woke up, he looked for the napkin with the number of the waitress who worked at the underground lounge. Next to the number read "Mention Cairo." He saw that the phone number didn't have an Atlanta area code and became curious. Is it her number? Does she not live in Atlanta? He dialed the number.

"Is this Cairo?" Percy asked.

"Who's this?" a man answered.

"It's Percy."

"Percy."

"I was told to mention Cairo," Percy said. "I'm from Atlanta."

"Cairo is my daughter," the man said.

"May I ask who I am talking to?"

"You may."

"Who am I talking to?" Percy asked.

"This is Jacques. I own a specialty Cajun store in New Orleans. It's a distributing company—trying to spread the love of Cajun food across the country."

Percy smiled. He made a connection and almost shouted in excitement.

"By any chance do you know Macy Thorpewaite?"

"Sure I do," said Jacques. "She was an old friend of mine from school. She helped Cairo out when she moved to Atlanta."

In his head, Percy thanked Macy.

"Well Jacques," Percy said. "I was a good friend of Macy, and somehow, through your daughter, she managed to connect us."

"Why so?"

"I have this idea," Percy said. "A restaurant idea."

52

ATLANTA CHRONICLE

The Vase Is Back In Its Right Place

To Leo and Jennifer's surprise, the vase has been returned to their house. It was left on their front porch while Jennifer was at the grocery store. Jennifer immediately called Leo and he left work early to take a look at his most valuable possession.

When asked if they knew who had left it on the door, Leo says, "I don't know who did it, but I do have a clue as to who might have brought it back. Because the person chose to remain anonymous, I will not state any names. Thank you so much, and if you ever want to let me know that you were the one to return the vase, please know that your reward awaits you."

When asked about the situation, Chief of Police Jasper Barbs said, "We worked hard. We didn't have anything to do with it, but we worked hard."

53

Percy spent about two weeks in New Orleans. He was able to meet up with Jacques and talk about possibly opening up a boudin café in Atlanta, and he was glad to see that Jacques was willing to help.

"I'm all in," Jacques said. "We can certainly distribute to Atlanta. A lot of possibilities can happen."

"I would like to get a head start on it," Percy said. "I have lots of ideas and with your help, this can actually happen."

He pretended that he was a shrewd businessman and imagined that he was wearing a business suit. I really need to know how to fix a tie, he thought.

"So how do you know Cairo?" Jacques said.

"I don't really know her. I was at a place where Macy liked to spend her time and somehow got this phone number and was told to mention Cairo, and now I'm here."

"Oh that Macy," Jacques said. "She was always up to something. The world can be so small sometimes."

"Small."

Percy told Jacques that he would be traveling for a bit, but once he got back to Atlanta, he'd get in touch with him. He ate a few boudin links while they met and cherished every bite. He thought about

Macy and wished he could have thanked her in person. She was always looking after me, he thought, whether she showed it or not.

"This can be another adventure," Percy said.

After two weeks in New Orleans, Percy went to the airport and bought a nonstop ticket from New Orleans to Chicago.

He loved the airport scene. It was like a hotel lobby. There were all kinds of people coming and going. People from all over the world were all in one place. He sat at the gate and watched the people walk by. Some looked tired. Others looked refreshed. There were business people doing business on their cell phones as they walked to their gates. It was just like a hotel lobby, but a lot larger.

He sat in the lobby and watched the people come and go as he listened to the jazz CD. It was almost surreal. Everything seemed to be in slow motion. He watched a lady wait for an arrival, and he watched her run to her husband or boyfriend as he walked through one of the gates. He had brought her some flowers. An old lady sat down next to Percy. She started saying something to him, but he couldn't hear her because he had headphones on. He took them off.

"Sorry?" Percy said.

"Looks like the flight is on time," she said.

She didn't sound too happy.

"I had a six-hour layover the other day because of the weather. I don't think I could wait for that long anymore."

"Live in Chicago?" Percy asked.

She had relatives there. She lived in New Orleans and worked for a company that had something to do with tourism. She was in a bad mood.

"What are you going to be doing in Chicago?" she asked.

"I don't know," Percy said. "But I have something of an idea. I do want to get a hot dog."

"A hot dog? You're going to Chicago to get a hot dog?"

"With relish."

He put on his headphones again. She said something, but he didn't bother trying to understand her. He kept listening to the jazz CD.

He turned his head to look at the others who were sitting at the Gate 18-A lobby. He saw a television attached to one of the pillars—he walked toward it. The television was pretty high, so when Percy approached it, he had to tilt his head upwards quite a bit. It was the Antique Roadshow. He couldn't hear what they were saying because the volume was turned off. He looked around but no one else was watching the show. He stood on a chair and looked at the screen. The item that was on display was a model ship in a casing. Next to the host was Barlow. He looked completely different. He looked younger, and his eyes were soft and watery. They were no longer the scorn-filled eyes he had seen when he first came to Atlanta. He wore a suit and a tie. Percy couldn't believe it—he shook his head and laughed and went back to his seat.

A few minutes later, the flight attendant made the announcement that the nonstop flight to Chicago was about to begin boarding. He smiled as he stood in line to board. He thought about Macy. He thought about Monica and Allen and he was already looking forward to seeing them again whenever he eventually decided to go back to Atlanta. He thought about the time he broke into the antique store. He thought about all of his past adventures, and the M.M.C., and how he was looking forward to more adventures in the future. He thought about boudin. And he thought about Chicago and finding Penelope and getting down on one knee to ask her out on a date.

Thank You

The Muu-Antiques couldn't have been created without the support, love, and care of the following lovely beings:

Thank you to my friends, who without hesitation have always shown so much kindness and support—your friendship means so much, truly and sincerely.

Thank you, Mike Bourgeois and Andy LeGoullon—thank you so much, for everything. Thank you, Chad and Bianca Cosby. Thank you, Karl Schott and Mandy Migues. Thank you, Rien Fertel. Thank you, Luke Sonnier. Thank you, Lindsey Sonnier. Thank you, Patrick O'Neil. Thank you, Jennifer Ames. Thank you, Jerome Moroux. Thank you, Katie Culbert. Thank you, Story Frantzen, Jacob Camden, and Abby Langford. Thank you, Jenny Melanson and Bullard Jones. Thank you, Leonard Chang. Thank you, Toby LeBlanc. Thank you, Rob Roberge. Thank you, Mathew Yates. Thank you, Priya Doraswamy. Thank you, Lafayette Barnes & Noble.

Many thanks to the Literary Community who has provided so much encouragement.

Thank you, Malarkey Books—for all of this.

And to my parents, Sarmistha and Subrata Dasgupta, my brother, Deep and my sister-in-law, Heidi—I love you all so much. Thank you, always, for being there. Love.

About the Author

Shome Dasgupta's novel *The Seagull And The Urn* was published by HarperCollins India, and it was also republished by Hachette/Headline Accent in the UK, and his experimental novella, *i am here And You Are Gone* won the 2010 OW Press Contest. His books include the novels *Tentacles Numbing* (Thirty West) and *Cirrus Stratus* (Spuyten Duyvil), an experimental book of prose, *Spectacles* (Word West), and a poetry collection, *Iron Oxide* (Assure Press). His writing has appeared in *McSweeney's Internet Tendency*, *Jabberwock Review*, *New Orleans Review*, *New Delta Review*, *Necessary Fiction*, *American Book Review*, *Arkansas Review*, *Magma Poetry*, and elsewhere. His fiction and poetry have also been anthologized in *Best Small Fictions* (Sonder Press), *The &Now Awards 2: The Best Innovative Writing* (&Now Books), and *Poetic Voices Without Borders 2* (Gival Press). His work has been featured as a *storySouth* Million Writers Award Notable Story, and his stories and poems have been nominated for the Pushcart Prize, Best Small Fictions, Best Of The Net, Best Microfiction, and the *Orison* Anthology.

He lives in Lafayette, LA, and can be found online at shomedome.com and @laughingyeti.

Other Titles from Malarkey Books

Faith, a novel by Itoro Bassey

The Life of the Party Is Harder to Find Until You're the Last One Around, poems by Adrian Sobol

Music Is Over, a novel by Ben Arzate

Toadstones, stories by Eric Williams

Deliver Thy Pigs, a novel by Joey Hedger

It Came From the Swamp, an anthology of stories featuring cryptids (aka bigfoot and mermaids and other legendary creatures), edited by Joey Poole

Pontoon, an anthology of fiction and poetry

What I Thought of Ain't Funny

Guess What's Different, essays by Susan Triemert

White People on Vacation, a novel by Alex Miller

Your Favorite Poet, poems by Leigh Chadwick,

Sophomore Slump, poems by Leigh Chadwick

Man in a Cage, a novel by Patrick Nevins

Fearless, a novel by Benjamin Warner

Don Bronco's (Working Title) Shell, a novel? by Donald Ryan

Un-ruined, a novel by Roger Vaillancourt

Thunder From a Clear Blue Sky, a novel by Justin Bryant

Kill Radio, a novel by Lauren Bolger

The Muu-Antiques, a novel by Shome Dasgupta

Gloria Patri, a novel by Austin Ross

Where the Pavement Turns to Sand, stories by Sheldon Birnie

Coming in 2024

Still Alive, a novel by LJ Pemberton
Thumbsucker, poems by Kat Giordano
Hope and Wild Panic, stories bySean Ennis
Sleep Decades, stories by Israel A. Bonilla
I Blame Myself But Also You (and Other Stories),
by Spencer Fleury
The Great Atlantic Highway & Other Stories,
by Steve Gergley
First Aid for Choking Victims,
stories by Matthew Zanoni Müller

malarkeybooks.com

www.ingramcontent.com/pod-product-compliance
Lightning Source LLC
Chambersburg PA
CBHW020124310726
48970CB00006B/1714